Murder at the
Blue Swan

A Novel

Billy Burnes

It gave me a strange feeling, and the rest of that night I didn't say much, but merely sat there and drank, trying to decide if I was getting older and wiser, or just plain old.

- Hunter S. Thompson; The Rum Diary

1

I finished the beer, tossed the empty can into the back seat, and turned up the windshield wipers. I had told myself I wasn't going to drink on the way home, but the empty road and the endless Pacific Ocean on my left made me feel lonely, and it was too damn quiet not to have a drink. My mind wandered to the image of a man's body floating face down in a pool. The blood spreading from his body like an underwater storm cloud tinged the water a dark red.

A car horn and a flash of headlights snapped me out of my thoughts, and I swerved back into my lane. I glanced in the rearview mirror at the car speeding in the opposite direction and caught a glimpse of my reflection. The cut above my eye was bruised and menacing. To hell with it, I thought. Maybe another beer would help me cope with the events of the past few weeks.

I grabbed a can from the six-pack sitting in the passenger seat, cracked it open, and felt lucky to be heading home.

The old saying goes, keep your friends close and your enemies closer. But what if you can't tell friend from foe? What if the people you thought you could rely on are actually hiding in the reeds, ready to strike? Who can you trust when your back is turned and the lights flicker out?

I had been sent to the Mexican border to write about life caught between two countries. My objective was to document the triumph of leaving the past behind to start fresh in a new world with new opportunities. The story was supposed to be filled with tales of second chances and dreams achieved. But the traumas of the past cannot always be outrun. The repercussions set in motion from a history of corruption leave wounds that fester and become scars.

Among the stories of transients and broken homes, I found examples of heartbreak and triumph, love and terror, and hope and death. The people caught between a dream ahead and a reality behind were being stripped of their identities and persecuted by the happenstance of their birthplace. They either ran with wild abandon or moved around like zombies. They were either late to be somewhere or had nowhere to go.

By the third or fourth day, I realized I didn't want to write about the crying mothers who were in constant prayer or the lonely children who peeked around corners. So I drank tequila and smoked cheap cigars. I slept on the ground and on crowded couches, and sometimes we hid or ran for no apparent reason. I lived with the people but watched them through the bottom of a tequila bottle and with the security granted by my birth nation. We laughed and cried and drank until the days blurred together and my emotions ran numb.

After days of heavy drinking, I was too erratic and fragile to write clearly, so I left the border without finishing the story. I crawled out of my hole and headed for the Pacific Ocean. But as I drove away, a memory of beauty began to blossom in my mind—that amidst the corruption and deceit of the border, there was a hidden sense of togetherness that ran through its veins if you dug deep enough. There was a mutual understanding among its people that dictated the terms of their relationships: trust only yourself, but help when you can.

It was the people I met after leaving the border who scared me the most. They lived by their own rules, disguising their deceit and hatred in cocktail dresses and three-piece suits. Their mission in life was to climb over each other and then cut the rope for those below. There was no unity, no harmony, no peace—only unbridled ambition and the devastation it left in its wake.

If I could go back in time, I would have stayed at the border and drunk until I wandered out into the desert and disappeared under a sage bush. At least I could have held onto hope that there was something beautiful beyond the chaos of new beginnings. At least I could have dreamed of a kinder world where people are what they seem, and this whole human experience isn't just a waste of time.

2

One week earlier

I pulled off the freeway into Point Loma around noon. It was Saturday afternoon, and the streets bustled with activity. A young mom and dad held their daughter's hands and swung her into the air as they crossed the street. The sun was radiant, the air felt crisp, and the hangover that had chased me from the border was no longer blinding.

I drove down Rosecrans Street to the end of the Point Loma peninsula, searching for my motel. The internet described it as a 1950s bungalow nestled in the heart of a beautiful San Diego beach town. It claimed to offer the charm of the American Dream for a price you could afford, but all I really needed was a strong drink and a soft bed.

The sign hanging from the front of the motel caught my attention first. It read "Blue Swan Motel" in such vibrant neon blue that it dulled the afternoon sunshine. There was a small garden out front filled with cacti and succulents, and big floor-to-ceiling windows looking into the lobby. I parked under two palm trees and a row of bamboo shoots that shielded the motel from prying eyes and hostile locals.

Inside, the lobby was small and quiet. A bench of cushions sat against the windows, and there was a shelf at the end with board games and books. The lobby opened up to the restaurant and bar, but it was too early for either to be inhabited by regal alcoholics. I approached the clerk at the front desk and gave him my name. He was a young guy about my age, but he looked at me warily, as if I were one of the bums or hippies standing on the street corners. I smiled at him to ease his nerves, but that seemed to make him even more squeamish.

He said my room wouldn't be ready until 3 p.m. and that I could wait by the pool. I asked him if there was any place nearby that served good bloody marys, and his mouth started to twitch uncontrollably. Apparently, the thought of me and booze conjured a frightening vision that his nerves couldn't handle. He finally skirted the question by replying that there were lots of places with good lunch menus.

I got back in my car, a '94 white Jeep Grand Cherokee with about a million miles on it, and drove to the closest pub I could find. It had a giant American flag hanging from the ceiling and strange paintings of tiny men on horseback on the walls. I ignored the little men with their permanently sly smiles and grabbed the last open spot at the bar.

The bartender was a young blonde girl with bright eyes and a warm smile. I hoped she was working her way through college and hadn't committed herself to a lifetime in the industry. I ordered a bloody mary, and she handed me a round wooden token along with the drink.

"What's this for?" I asked.

"It's a bar promotion," she answered cheerfully. "Every drink comes with a token and a chance to win a pony."

I thought I heard her wrong.

"A pony?" I asked, skeptical that the past few days of heavy drinking had damaged my sense of hearing or grip on reality.

"Yes, you win a pony," she repeated as if it were obvious.

"As in a miniature horse?"

"Yep."

"A real, live one?"

Her eyebrows lowered like she was concerned about my questioning. "Do you want a dead one?"

"No," I answered. "But I'm not sure I want a live one either."

Her look of concern vanished with a chuckle. "You can choose to win a pony keg of beer if you don't want the real pony. The drawing is scheduled for September first, two weeks from today. You have to be here in person to win if your ticket is pulled."

I shook my head in disbelief. "I've spent the past ten years of my life in every kind of bar you can imagine. This is the first time I've seen a live animal raffled off as a promotion. I kind of pity the animal that has to go live with an alcoholic who has no experience raising large animals."

The bartender nodded in agreement. "I think that too. Hopefully, whoever wins knows what they're doing or chooses the pony keg."

"Where's the pony now?" I asked, taking a sip of the bloody mary. It was strong and spicy, and I knew I'd order more.

The bartender shrugged. "I'm not sure. Some farm outside of the city."

I imagined bringing a pony home to the small, one-bedroom apartment I shared with my girlfriend. I could ride it through the front door and say I'd found the solution to my problem of drinking on the road. Then I wondered which one of us my girlfriend would kick to the street.

"How do I win?" I asked, more than a little intrigued by the image of myself sitting atop the pony.

The bartender pointed to a miniature basketball hoop attached to the wall above the bar. "Every token gives you a chance to shoot in the hoop. If you make it in the hoop, you get a ticket. If your ticket is pulled on the day of the drawing, you win the pony."

I picked up the small wooden token from the bartop. It had the profile of an old sailor etched into one side. "When do I shoot?"

"You can shoot now," she said, "or wait till you're done drinking and shoot all at once."

"I might be drinking for a while," I said. "This is a damn good bloody mary."

The bartender laughed. "Best in the city. And they're bottomless until 2 p.m."

I told her to keep the bloody marys coming and that I'd try a couple of shots right now. She mixed me another drink and gave me another token. I slid both tokens across the bar, and she handed me a small plastic basketball. I walked to the middle of the bar and stood behind a couple of guys sitting in front of the hoop. When they didn't acknowledge my apology for invading their space, I decided to take my shots without their consent.

My first shot ricocheted off the wall and landed harmlessly behind the bar. The bartender retrieved it and passed it to me over the two guys. The ball flying over their heads caught their attention.

"Hey, Kayci, we want another shot too," one of them barked. He was a middle-aged guy wearing a sports jersey and a backwards hat. He had a pitcher of beer in front of him. I figured he was one of those guys who went to college just to party and then got an office job after graduation, but could never give up the college lifestyle.

"You guys don't have any more shots, Jesse," Kayci replied. Her voice carried only the slightest hint of annoyance.

"Come on," Jesse begged, pointing his thumb at me over his shoulder. "You let this guy shoot, but not us."

"He paid for his drinks and gets to shoot just like everyone else," Kayci said. Then she looked back at me. "Go ahead and shoot your shot."

This time, I aimed for the middle of the backboard and put more touch on the shot. The ball bounced softly off the wall and fell through the net. Kayci ripped a yellow ticket off a roll and reached between the two guys to hand it to me.

Jesse thrust out his hand, trying to swipe it from her. Kayci quickly pulled it back and glared at him. "Are you going to let me give this man his ticket?" There was no amusement in her voice.

Jesse held out his hand expectantly. "Only if you give me another shot."

Kayci shook her head, looked at me again, and nodded toward the other end of the bar. "Meet me down by your seat."

I followed her back to my stool, and she handed me the ticket. "Come back on the first if you want to be in the drawing."

Jesse stood up on the footrest of his stool and watched our exchange. "Hey, buddy," he shouted over the other patrons sitting at the bar.

I ignored him and took a sip of my bloody mary.

"Hey, buddy," he shouted again. "How about you give me that ticket and I'll buy you a drink?" He continued standing on his stool, glaring over everyone like he was the king of the bar.

I waited a moment longer, then looked over and made eye contact with him. "I think I'll hold on to it," I said.

Jesse didn't like my response. His face turned red, and he puffed out his chest. "I've never seen you here before. This is my bar. I'm going to be here for the ticket drawing. Are you?"

"You seem to really want that pony," I replied.

Jesse's face twisted into a snarl. "Answer the question, bro."

"OK, fine," I said. "I probably won't be here, but it's weird that a grown man wants a little horse so badly."

Jesse's barstool scraped across the floor as he jumped down. "What the hell did you just say to me?"

The guy next to Jesse wrapped an arm around his chest. "Come on, Jesse," he urged. "It's not worth it."

Jesse squirmed in his friend's grasp. "No. I want to know who this guy thinks he is, that he can come in here and talk to me like that."

Kayci walked back over to them. "OK, Jesse. I think you've had enough. It's time to go." She grabbed the half-empty pitcher of beer in front of him and set it behind the bar.

"What the hell!" Jesse cried. "You can't treat me like this. I'm a regular. This is my bar."

Jesse's friend kept his arm around Jesse's chest and dragged him away from the bar. Jesse cursed and wriggled like a child, but didn't put any real effort into escaping his friend's grip. They backed out the door, and the friend pushed Jesse toward the street. The rest of the patrons at the bar burst into laughter when the door closed behind them. It seemed that Jesse wasn't well-liked, even as a regular at his bar.

Kayci walked back over to me with a thin smile. "Sorry, man. He isn't a bad guy, just has a drinking problem."

"It's no problem," I said. "I know about drinking problems."

She placed an upside-down shot glass in front of me. "If you want anything to drink besides bloody marys, it's on the house."

I thanked her, and she walked away seemingly unfazed by the entire ordeal. I sat at the bar for a few more hours, drinking bloody marys and watching the locals. A guy wearing a shirt and tie came in, clapped everyone on the back, and called them by name. He didn't even sit down; he just ordered a shot, downed it, and left. One guy sat at the end of the bar with a newspaper and a drink, not moving the entire time. I wanted to ask what he was reading, but he never looked up from the paper.

It was 3 p.m. when I paid my tab and decided to forgo my remaining shots for the pony. I had drunk a gallon of bloody marys but forgot to order something to eat. My stomach felt wretched, and my feet dragged on the floor. I handed the pony ticket to a family of four sitting at a table by the door. The dad looked at me like I was a lunatic, but was too polite to refuse the ticket.

I drove back to the Blue Swan and almost parked neatly within the lines of a single parking spot. The same clerk was sitting behind the front desk. His expression sank when he saw me stumble through the door. I was about to tell him that his face was interfering with his job of ensuring customer satisfaction, but I refrained. After all, I was a professional and couldn't cause fright among the staff so early in my stay.

The cushioned benches along the wall looked tantalizingly comfortable, but I knew that if I lay down, the clerk would badger me relentlessly and prevent any attempt at undisturbed sleep. He handed me a room key, pointed me toward the door, and asked if he could help me to my room. I assured him I was competent enough to find the room myself since the motel was just a two-story building with fewer than twenty rooms. A minute later, I fumbled the key trying to unlock the door, dropped my bag on the floor when I finally managed to get in, and face-planted onto the bed.

3

I woke up a little after 7 p.m. The fading sunlight seeped through the open window, and the cool air promised a beautiful night on the coast. I sat up and teetered on the edge of the bed for a minute. The taste of bloody marys coated my mouth and stomach; my bones creaked from exhaustion and poor decisions.

I went to the bathroom to clean up and wash my face. The reflection in the mirror looked like me in twenty years. I splashed some water on my face and looked back in the mirror, but the reflection didn't change.

Back in the bedroom, I turned on the local news while getting dressed. The weather forecaster said there was a storm at sea that would bring strong wind gusts and a massive swell for a couple of days. The surfers were going to have a heyday, but the land dwellers could rest easy knowing there wouldn't be a cloud in the beautiful Southern California sky.

I put on my least wrinkled clothes—tan slacks and a black polo shirt—slipped the room key into my wallet, and left the room. I hadn't been in the right mindset earlier to survey the motel while crawling up the stairs in a bloody mary paralysis. The motel was shaped like a rectangular horseshoe. My room was tucked away in a corner on the second floor. In the middle of the horseshoe was a courtyard with a pool and dining tables scattered around the deck. The restaurant opened to the courtyard through large sliding glass doors. The doors were open now, and Frank Sinatra's voice filled the courtyard.

I walked down the stairs and through the lobby to the bar. A few customers sat at tables, talking over martinis and old fashioneds. A waitress was hanging streamers above the bar, and another was talking with a DJ, who was leaning against his turntable. I sat down in the middle of the bar and waited for the bartender. The bartop was long and made of dark marble. It was clean and fancy and felt like a good place to enjoy a healthy night.

"Got a party going on tonight?" I asked the bartender when he came over. He was wearing a white shirt and a black tie. His sleeves were rolled up to his elbows, showing off faded tattoos on both arms.

"Corporate party tonight," he replied. "They wanted the full package and all the glitz and glam that comes with it."

I checked my watch; it was nearly 8 p.m. "They must be coming in hot if they aren't here yet."

The bartender leaned against the bar and looked past me toward the windows in the lobby. "Well, they paid for an open bar starting at seven, whether they show up or not. In the meantime, can I get you anything to drink?"

The thought of alcohol made my throat constrict. "I'll be sticking to water tonight. Thank you, though."

"You sure? If you say you're a member of the party, then it's on the house. Or, technically, on your employer's tab." He smiled as if he were sharing a secret with old friends. Maybe he was bored, or maybe he just liked sticking it to the man.

Despite my inhibitions, refusing a free drink was akin to slapping a gift out of someone's hands. It was rude, undignified, and went against my deeply held personal credo. "I'll take a whiskey neat," I said. "And an order of chicken alfredo."

"Yes, sir," the bartender said triumphantly. He poured me a drink and placed my food order. "My name's Tim, if you need anything else."

I busied myself with my drink until a food runner brought out my dinner and placed it in front of me. I ate peacefully, trying not to spy too much on the other patrons. A middle-aged couple sat at the end of the bar, laughing and touching each other like they were on a second date. A single man sat sullenly at the other end of the bar. He was shaggy-looking and probably hadn't been on a date in years.

I'd just finished eating when the party arrived. They spilled out of a party bus like an army battalion storming a beach. They came to the bar loud and thirsty. A couple of girls shoved up next to me and called for the bartender. They looked to be in their mid-twenties, not much younger than me, but they made me feel old. They were dressed in tight skirts and plunging necklines. They knew they looked good, and they knew how to have a good time.

I accidentally made eye contact with one of them. She smiled at me with sparkling teeth and drunken eyes. Her hair was black; her skin was a soft brown. "Hi," she said. "Are you partying tonight also?"

"The party might be over for me tonight," I said, lifting my glass off the bar to show her it was empty.

"What? Why? Come on! The party is just getting started." She rattled off her words in rapid fire, the pitch in her voice rising with each one.

Before I could respond, a guy came over and draped his arm around her shoulder. "Who's taking shots!" he shouted. It was more of an exclamation than a question. He was wearing a light blue three-piece suit, but his tie was loose and his collar was undone. I assumed his blonde hair was usually perfectly manicured, but it was ruffled now. His piercing blue eyes were full of energy and liquor.

The bartender poured four shots of tequila for the group and looked at me while holding the bottle over another shot glass. "Come on, man," the young man urged. "No one drinks alone."

I hesitated; this wasn't part of my plan for the evening. But maybe it was my damn rule about accepting free drinks that swayed me, or maybe it was their collective belief that if they were partying, then everyone else had to be partying too. So I said yes. The girls cheered, and the guy clapped loudly in victory.

"Here's to you, here's to me, here's to making lots of money," he sang as we clinked glasses. I thought it was an awkward salute, though the girls didn't seem to mind. They all slammed down their glasses like they had just won a game.

"Where's Charlie at?" the guy said, turning away from the bar and looking out toward the pool. Apparently, he spotted the person he was looking for because he took off with the same hyped-up energy he came over with. Two of the girls went with him.

The girl who asked me if I was partying stayed behind. She smiled at me again, this time somewhat awkwardly. "That's Jordan. He's getting a big promotion, and our boss is paying for his celebration." She paused for a split second. "His dad is our boss."

She had strangely calmed down after taking the shot. Either the tequila was her fix, or her act left when her friends did. "What's your name?" she asked and reached out her hand to me.

I shook her hand. "I'm Billy."

"Nice to meet you, Billy. I'm Jackie," she said, pulling her hand back and resting her chin on it.

"It's nice to meet you, Jackie. I'm guessing this isn't your first stop for the night."

"No, it's not. We had dinner at an Italian restaurant. But we didn't eat much. We mostly just drank." Her eyes never left me as she talked. I couldn't tell if she was studying me or just being friendly, but it made me a little nervous being the object of her attention.

"And your boss paid for all of it?" I asked. "The company must be doing well."

"Yes, it is. But I just answer the phone and set up meetings." She didn't sound upset despite her disparaging words about her position.

"What type of company do you answer the phone for?" I asked.

"Real estate," she answered proudly. "We sell some of the most high-end homes in the San Diego area."

"Well, what a coincidence. I'm actually looking to buy a high-end home in the area," I lied.

"Really? Well, then, this is your lucky night," Jackie said, and laughed. She could probably see right through my facade.

"On second thought, I'm fine with a meager two-bedroom apartment, on account of all the cleaning, ya know?"

Jackie laughed again. "No one who owns a big home actually cleans it themselves."

Tim came over and asked if we wanted another round. I ordered another whiskey, and Jackie ordered a martini. I thought she was too young to drink martinis, but then again, I never had much class. We sat in silence while Tim poured the drinks, both of us watching the people laughing and dancing around the bar without a care in the world. I figured that money really could buy happiness, even if only for a night.

"So, what does Jordan do for the company?" I asked once Tim had finished pouring our drinks and moved on to the next group of patrons.

"Well, he's sort of the lead agent now. He gets first call on all the big listings." She paused, and her eyes twinkled. "But I want to know about you, Billy. What brings you here tonight?"

I shrugged because there was nothing worth telling. "I have a room here for the night. It was quiet this afternoon. I took a nap, came down for dinner, and was just finishing up when you guys rolled in."

"Oh. So we ruined a quiet night for you?" she said playfully, giving me a sarcastic look to show she knew they weren't really ruining my night.

I figured it wouldn't hurt to play along. "Something like that. But quiet isn't always good." The whiskey and tequila mixture was warming my insides and reviving my mood.

Jackie raised her glass. "Cheers to that," she laughed. It was a joyful laugh that made me want to join in.

I raised my glass to hers, and we both took a hefty sip of our drinks.

"What do you do, Billy?" she asked once she set her glass down and let the taste dissipate. "Like, for a living, I mean?"

"I write for a magazine," I answered.

"Ooo," she drawled, tilting her chin and looking at me out of the corner of her eye. "Have you written anything I've read?"

"Probably not. We're a small news magazine in Sacramento."

"What's it called?"

"*The California Independent.*"

"So you're like a news reporter?" It was obvious she hadn't heard of our magazine. Not many people had, even in Sacramento.

"My editor calls me an investigative journalist."

"Oh, I like that," she said with another smile. "What does it mean?"

"It means they send me all over the state to write about events or people my editor finds interesting."

"That sounds like fun. I bet you're good at it."

Her unfounded compliment made me feel phony, considering my past week of debauchery and waste. I tried to hide my discomfort behind my drink and glanced again at the party picking up around us. The DJ had begun playing a deep, pounding beat through the speakers. It wasn't my style, but it matched the party and the vibe of the night. Everyone looked good. Everyone looked intoxicated. Servers moved through them like quiet assassins, constantly fueling the beast that was taking hold of the night.

Jackie asked if I wanted to join her on the patio, and I followed her to a table by the pool. Jordan, the other girls from the bar, and a guy who must have been Charlie were sitting at the table with full drinks and empty shot glasses in front of them. Charlie's hair was parted and gelled, his goatee was well-groomed, and he was wearing a white dress shirt with black suspenders. His attire suited the occasion, but his eyes darted around warily, like he was expecting trouble.

"Hey, guys. This is Billy," Jackie said to introduce me to the group. "He wanted a quiet night before we got here, but he's having a better night now that we've shown up."

The two girls said hello. Jordan looked at me with a drunken grin. His hair was more disheveled than it had been just a few minutes earlier. "What's up, Billy?" he said pompously. "Are you here to drink all of our alcohol?"

I wasn't sure if it was a joke or not. Charlie laughed, though, then stopped when no one else did. Jordan noticed my slow reaction. "I'm just kidding, man. Everyone is welcome to the party."

A waitress weaved through the group and placed a large bowl of fruit in front of Jordan. "Yes! Finally!" he shouted. "Now, the real fun can begin."

He sat upright in his chair, reached down to his right, and lifted a long wooden tube. He placed the tube on the table and, with a hand on each end, yanked it apart. The sword he now held in his right hand looked sleek and sharp. He stared at the blade as he sliced it through the air. The look in his eyes was evil, like the eyes of a lonely boy in the woods, skinning a squirrel for fun. He stood up suddenly with a burst of energy. The surrounding group, including myself, flinched backward in response.

"Do you guys know what this is?" he asked everyone.

No one answered.

"This is a samurai's katana," he answered himself. "An ancient killing machine used to gut and decapitate their enemies." He stabbed the air in slow motion to demonstrate its lethal properties. "Who wants to throw the fruit?" he asked, his eyes darting around the group gathered by the table.

There was a stunned silence. Even Charlie, who probably knew about the sword, shied away from Jordan's challenge. I looked around to see if the restaurant staff had witnessed the escalation in the night, but they didn't seem aware of the barbaric weapon slicing through the tranquility of their motel.

"Come on," Jordan growled. "It's my party. Someone is going to throw me some goddamn fruit." He looked at Charlie, whose chair was noticeably a few inches further from the table. "Let's go, Charlie. Grab an apple."

Charlie frowned at the bowl of fruit and tugged at his ear-lobe. Jordan didn't notice. He was whipping chairs away from the pool, creating a zone of terror for himself. Charlie glanced from the fruit bowl to the rest of the group for reassurance. Everyone returned his glance; no one offered assistance.

"Charlie, let's go!" Jordan barked again.

Charlie took a deep breath, then chugged the rest of his beer. He stood up, grabbed a handful of fruit from the bowl, and walked toward the pool. The thump of the DJ's music followed his steps like background music in a movie.

Jordan waited at the edge of the pool, his legs bent in an athletic stance. He wasn't smiling anymore; his face was tense, and his eyes were manic. He gripped the handle of the sword as if he were trying to squeeze it into dust. He was coiled energy, ready to spring forth and wreak havoc.

Charlie positioned himself a few feet in front of Jordan. "Big one first. Don't miss," he said, trying to sound playful. He held up an apple for Jordan to see.

Jordan was not in the mood for jokes. He raised the handle of the sword above his head. "Throw the fucking fruit, bro," he said coldly.

Charlie tossed the apple underhand. Jordan let out his imi-tation of a samurai shriek and took a step forward, bringing the blade down like a guillotine. Two clean-cut halves of apple fell to the ground. One of them rolled under the table, the other into the pool. The crowd around Jordan sat in stunned silence at the display of bravado and absurdity.

Jordan must have expected a celebration, though, because he looked around like a child seeking approval. "Come on!" he shouted, pumping the sword toward the sky in a vain attempt to hype up the crowd.

"Cut something smaller if you're good," a guy in the outer ring of the crowd called out. Everyone turned to look at him. He was a tall man with dark, slicked-back hair and yellow-tinted glasses. The corner of his mouth was turned up in a smirk. He looked like someone from a movie, but I couldn't put my finger on who.

"That's a great fucking idea, Matt," Jordan said, thrusting his finger in Matt's direction. "That's why I fucking love you, man. And that's why you're going to be right there with me on this new mission."

Matt shook his head in response, but the smirk didn't leave his face.

"Come on, Charlie," Jordan said. "Get me something smaller."

Charlie returned to the fruit bowl and fished out a strawberry. He again tossed the fruit underhand into the air, and Jordan once again sliced it cleanly in half. This time, the crowd cheered without any prompting.

I excused myself from the group and headed back to the bar. I had no interest in watching a man-child beg for attention on a night already dedicated to his promotion. A couple of restaurant staff hurried past me toward the pool, finally noticing the deranged man swinging a sword in their establishment. By the time I reached the bar, Jordan was shouting that this was his party and that his money bought him the right to do whatever he goddamn pleased.

4

The party continued into the night. Jackie and I were sitting at the bar when she paused our conversation and pointed toward the door. A large middle-aged man was strolling into the lobby with a woman at least half his age on his arm. He was tall with the chest of a bull and the demeanor of a lion. She was thin and blonde, with the air of a movie star. He was dressed in an all-black suit; she was wearing a sparkling white minidress. Her lipstick was such a vibrant red against her light skin and blonde hair that it bewitched the eyes like a visual siren's song.

"That's Mr. Carter and his wife, Jaselle," Jackie whispered as if it were a secret, but everyone else had also noticed Mr. and Mrs. Carter's arrival.

"She looks much younger than him," I said, and then hoped it wasn't rude to say.

"She is," Jackie continued to whisper. "By about thirty years. But Mr. Carter is not your typical older man. You'll see."

The couple strutted up to the bar like they owned the motel. "Scotch for me," Carter ordered. "Vodka tonic for her." His voice was commanding and final. I got the impression that he was used to getting his way all the time.

Carter noticed Jackie sitting at the bar. "Hello, Jackie," he said in a deep voice. "I hope the night is treating you well."

"Hi, Mr. Carter. It's a great night. Thank you," she replied. Then she looked at Jaselle. "Hi, Jaselle. Your dress is beautiful."

"Thank you, Jackie," Jaselle said. Her voice was delicate, like it could be carried away on a gentle breeze. "You look stunning tonight, as always."

"How was dinner?" Carter asked, cutting between the two women.

"Great. The restaurant was wonderful, and the food was delicious," Jackie lied.

Tim finished pouring the couple's drinks, and Carter slid a crisp hundred-dollar bill across the bar. I thought it was an odd exchange, since Tim had said the drinks were already paid for.

"And my son?" Carter asked, raising his eyebrows. "Is he behaving himself tonight?"

Jackie hesitated, maybe deliberating how much to reveal about Jordan's massacre of the fruit. "He is having fun," she answered safely.

Carter gave a knowing grunt. "I think my son having fun may not be enjoyable for everyone else." He wrapped an arm around Jaselle's waist and kissed her on the cheek. She giggled and looked at him adoringly. I figured their marriage was new, and they were still fooling each other.

Jordan appeared behind his father from out of the crowd. "Hello, Mr. Carter," he said, grabbing his father's shoulders and giving them a little shake. "I'm glad to see the old man decided to come out tonight. The fun is just picking up." His grip on his father could have been mistaken for a sign of affection, except that he kept an arm's distance between the two of them.

Carter took his time as he turned around and leaned back on the bar. His eyes narrowed as he looked his son up and down.

I couldn't tell if he liked what he saw. Jordan took a step back and tried to smile.

"Good evening, Jordan. You're not hogging the bar to yourself, are you?" Carter said jokingly, but his eyes were cold.

Jordan spread his hands and glanced around to show off the party. "Everyone is having a great time. Even Billy here is enjoying the party." He pointed at me with his chin as he said it. I instantly hated him even more.

Carter turned to look at me while still leaning back against the bar. He swirled the scotch in his glass as he sized me up. "Billy, I don't think you work for me, do you?"

I couldn't tell if it was a hostile question, so I answered honestly. "No, I do not. I'm just a lonely patron staying at the motel for the night."

Jackie jumped to my defense. "Billy was eating dinner when we got here. We sort of ambushed his quiet night."

Carter continued to stare at me with a knowing look. "A man only has a quiet night at a motel bar when he's got something on his mind or he's running from something."

"Oh, let him be, Ross," Jaselle said, playfully slapping Carter's chest. She looked over at me. "Don't worry, Ross is always trying to get inside your head. He thinks he can figure everyone out." She smiled as she spoke. It was a light, easy smile. I could see why a man would fall for her.

"It's OK," I responded. "He's not wrong."

Carter grunted. "I like a man who has things on his mind. It proves that he's more man than beast." He paused for a moment, then raised his chin and, still facing away from the bar, shouted, "Bartender! Get this man another drink!" Tim came over, and once again, I found myself with a glass full of whiskey at no cost to me.

An offshoot of the party recognized Mr. and Mrs. Carter at the bar and walked over to us, laughing loudly. The girls all hugged Jaselle and told her how beautiful she looked. They could have all been the same age. The guy in the group was the tall man Jordan had called Matt during the samurai escapade. He was several inches taller than everyone else. His yellow-tinged glasses gave him a devilish look that he must have enjoyed. We made eye contact, and his focus narrowed on me before he looked away, dismissing me as harmless.

Jackie grabbed one of the girls and dragged her over to our stools. "Leah, this is Billy. Billy, this is Leah." I wasn't sure if she was showing me off or Leah.

Leah had blonde hair, blue eyes, and a dress that revealed more skin than it covered. She looked like she could sell a man his own gravestone. "Hi, Leah. Nice to meet you," I said.

"The pleasure is mine, Billy." She turned to Jackie. "He's cute, Jackie," she added with an impish smile.

Jackie flashed the same mischievous grin. "I know."

I took a slug of my whiskey to settle the nerves that had surfaced from the girls' interaction. They must have recognized the expression on my face because they looked at each other and laughed.

"Oh, we made him nervous, Jackie," Leah said with a hint of satisfaction.

Jackie smiled at my nervousness as well. "It's cute. Billy is an investigative journalist for a magazine."

"I need to find me a Billy tonight," Leah said to Jackie as if I wasn't there. Then she returned her attention to me. "An investigative journalist sounds dangerous."

"It's not as adventurous as it sounds," I stammered. "It's mostly just sitting behind a desk or behind the steering wheel."

"What do you investigate?" she asked with a sly smile. "Murders?"

"Sometimes."

"Have you ever seen a dead body?"

"Leah!" Jackie shouted, swiping at the air in front of Leah. "I don't think he wants to talk about that right now."

Leah attempted an innocent shrug. "What? It's just a question."

"It's OK," I said. "I've seen a few. It's never a pleasant sight, but it gets easier, depending on the circumstances."

Leah flashed that impish grin again. "See? I knew you were a dangerous man."

Fortunately, Jordan rescued me from admitting that the only person I was dangerous to was myself. "Leah!" he shouted when he spotted her standing with us. "I've been looking for you!"

Leah's face lost its playful innocence and was replaced by blatant annoyance. "Yes, Jordan. I've been hiding from you."

"You play too much, Leah." He laughed and put an arm around Leah's shoulder, but she shrugged it off.

"Hands to yourself, Jordan," she said, looking at Jackie for help. Jackie didn't move but offered Leah an awkward smile of support.

"Come on," he pleaded. "Let's party tonight."

Leah looked around the bar for some sort of distraction. "We are partying, Jordan. Don't make it weird."

"It's not weird. Want a shot?"

"No, I don't. My drink is actually by the pool." She squeezed Jackie's arm as a farewell and left us with Jordan's bruised ego in her wake. I watched her join Matt at one of the tables. He leaned toward her and wrapped an arm around her waist. Leah let his hand rest there for a second before she softly patted it. Matt pulled his hand back, but Leah didn't leave.

"Aw, fuck it," Jordan said. He didn't acknowledge Jackie or me standing there as witnesses to his rejection. He spun around and wandered off toward whatever new shiny thing caught his attention.

"What was that all about?" I asked Jackie after he left.

Jackie shrugged off the awkward interaction. "Just office drama. It happens all the time. Come on, I could use another drink myself." She squeezed closer to me so she could lean over the bar and call for Tim. Tim hurried over, poured me a whiskey, and started on her martini.

"Is this your last stop for the night?" I asked.

"Yes, we already booked our rooms here for the night," she answered. "Some of us actually got ready here earlier before the party bus picked us up for dinner."

"That's pretty smart planning."

Jackie laughed. "What can I say? We know how to party."

"So, this is it—the final scene."

"Well, it is the end of the road, but it's not the end of the party," she replied with a sly smile that made me take a big gulp of whiskey.

The party grew heavier as the night wore on. Jackie introduced me to the rest of the group, and I tried to say something nice and remember each of their faces, but eventually, all the glitter and glam looked the same. They were still partying when a gut instinct told me to call it a night. I had learned long ago to run and hide when the party raged for too long. The last thing I remember was Jackie yelling goodnight from the pool deck as I stumbled up the stairs to my room.

5

I woke up in the middle of the night, soaked in cold sweat. It took a moment to remember I was in a motel in San Diego, five hundred miles from home. My head felt like it had been bucked off a bull and stomped into the ground. I rolled to the edge of the bed and turned on the lamp. The room lit up enough for me to spot my bag and shuffle over to it. The Advil bottle buried somewhere inside was the only substitute for whiskey to ease a headache. I found the bottle and turned it over, but nothing came out.

I sat back on the bed and dialed the number for the front desk. "Front desk," a woman's voice said after the second ring.

"Yes, hello," I stammered. "I'm in desperate need of some Advil. Do you keep any stocked in the motel?"

"Is everything OK, sir?" the woman asked.

"Yes, I just have a headache that could kill a pony," I answered.

"Right, can you... Oh my god." The woman paused for a moment. "I'm sorry, Mr. Burnes. It appears that one of the guests has decided to go for a late-night swim. If you can come down to the front desk, we have a bottle of Advil here."

I thanked her and hung up the phone. The digital clock on the bedside table showed 3:49 a.m. I grabbed my pants from the floor, flipped the doorstop, and left the room. The light in my corner of the hallway was dim, but the string of lights hanging above the courtyard created an ominous glow that drew me toward them like a moth to a flame.

I could hear someone shuffling around on the pool deck, and when I reached the railing, a woman was kneeling at the edge of the pool. Just out of her reach, a person was floating face down in the water. Something long and sleek was sticking out from the person's back, and the water around the body was tinted red, like someone had dumped a red lava lamp into the pool.

"Hey, what's going on?" I called down to the woman. My heart started beating faster as recognition began to set in.

My words startled the woman. She screamed, leaped up, and backed away from the pool. Her hands clutched her chest as if to stop her heart from tearing itself out of her body. "I don't know," she stuttered. "I thought he was swimming. But he's not moving." Her words came out in gasps. "And there's that thing in the middle of his back. What is it?"

I knew what it was, but she probably didn't want to hear the answer. I looked around to see if the woman's scream had woken anyone else, but the hallways were empty. All signs of life and foolishness from the party had been cleaned up and scrubbed away. It was almost like the party had never taken place at all, except for the body floating face down in the pool.

I hurried down the stairs and through the lobby. When I reached the pool, the woman was still standing there with the same frozen expression on her face. Her clothing indicated that she was the front desk clerk I had spoken to on the phone.

"Call the police," I said, then stepped around her and jumped into the pool.

I kicked over to the body, grabbed a fistful of shirt, and started pulling it toward the shallow end. The body bobbed in the water, resisting me as if it were angry at being disturbed from its slumber. When we finally reached the steps, I stepped onto the top one and reached under the arms. Then I heaved and tried to lift the body out of the water, but it was too heavy and splashed back down on the steps. I took a breath and heaved again. This time, the torso managed to flop onto the pool deck, but it was twisted and propped up against the foot of metal sticking out of its stomach.

Before I could finish hauling the rest of the body from the water, someone grabbed the legs and pulled them onto the deck. I didn't recognize the man who was now standing over the body, but I did recognize Jordan's face staring at me from beyond the grave. His eyes and mouth were open, like he was just as surprised as we were by the sword sticking through his gut.

"Oh shit," the man said, shuffling back from Jordan's body. "Is he alive?"

I crawled out of the pool and checked for a pulse in Jordan's neck, even though I knew there wouldn't be one. I slumped down next to the body and shook my head. My heart and lungs were pounding too hard to care about the cocktail of water and blood spreading across the pool deck and soaking into my pants.

"Jesus," the man said. "What happened?"

"I don't know," I panted.

One half of Jordan's samurai sword was sticking out of his back, and the other half was sticking out of his stomach. I imagined it would be a gruesome task for whoever was tasked with pulling the sword out of his body. Hopefully, it came out cleanly and didn't require grabbing the handle with both hands, placing one foot on the wall, and heaving it out.

"Is it just you down here?" the man asked, frantically scanning the shadows cast by the lights over the pool.

"The desk clerk was here before me. She's inside now, calling the police."

The man's eyes flicked back to me and narrowed. I couldn't tell if he was deciding whether I was the killer or if I needed to be killed. "You're sitting in blood," he said finally.

I scrambled up to my feet and scurried away from Jordan's limp body. My clothes were waterlogged and probably covered with traces of blood. Now that I had caught my breath, the thought of being covered in Jordan's blood made me want to burn my clothes and scrub my skin until it peeled off. "I need to get a towel and talk to the clerk," I said. The man nodded and followed me to the door.

As we were about to walk into the lobby, a woman's voice called from the railing above the pool. My heart sank. I turned around and saw Jackie standing over the railing. She was wearing a white bathrobe, her arms crossed tightly against her chest to ward off the night and any dangers it concealed.

"Billy, what's going on?" she asked tentatively. "Is that a person?" She couldn't see Jordan's face from her angle.

I didn't know what to say to her. We had only met a few hours ago, and I only remembered part of our conversation.

"Billy, is that a person?" she asked again, her voice trembling with growing anxiety.

"Jackie, I'm so sorry. It's Jordan."

"Oh my God," she gasped. "Oh my God. Is he dead?"

There was only one way to respond to the question. "Yes."

"Oh my God. Did he drown?"

"I don't think so. Someone put his sword clean through him."

"I can't believe this," Jackie stammered. "This isn't real. Did you call the cops?"

"The cops are on their way," I said, and a faint siren sounded in the distance, as if my words had brought it into existence. "Carter doesn't know yet. Is he staying here tonight?"

Jackie grabbed her head with both hands, and her robe slipped open. She didn't notice or care. "Yes, he is," she answered.

"Can you go wake him? The night clerk found Jordan in the pool, and I'd better go check on her."

Jackie said she would find Carter. She was about to turn away when she noticed the other guy standing by the lobby door. "Joe? Is that you?"

I looked again at the man who helped pull Jordan out of the pool. He was wearing black shorts and a black shirt. He had a grizzly beard that almost touched his chest.

"Jackie, I swear I had nothing to do with this," Joe said. He looked at the pool when he spoke rather than up to Jackie at the railing.

"What are you still doing here?" Jackie asked. She realized her robe had slipped open and pulled it tight around herself again.

Joe finally looked up at Jackie. "I couldn't sleep after the party," he said. "I heard someone scream, and I came out to check what was going on. I saw this guy jump into the pool and start pulling Jordan out of the water. So I ran down here to help. I didn't even realize it was Jordan until we had him out of the pool."

Jackie didn't respond when Joe finished his story. She stared at him like she was seeing a ghost, and Joe stared at her like he'd just been handed a life sentence.

"Jackie," I said to break the silence. "Go get Carter. I need to speak to the clerk."

Jackie broke her stare. "OK. I'll try calling him first." She went back into her room but left the door open.

I turned to Joe. "Joe, thank you for your help. Can you give the cops a statement when they arrive?"

Joe hesitated before responding. His eyes darted to Jordan and then quickly away. Finally, he nodded. "Yes. But right now, I need to check on my wife." Then he sprinted through the lobby and up the stairs.

I watched him leave and wondered why Jackie had been so surprised to see him. I looked down one last time at Jordan's body, twisted on its side with the sword protruding from his back and stomach. The night was silent now. It felt like it was just me, Jordan's lifeless body, and the quiet stars a thousand miles above.

6

The clerk was trembling behind the front desk like a puppy in a shelter when I walked into the lobby. I approached her slowly, trying to avoid any sudden movements.

"Hi," I said in the calmest voice possible, given the circumstances. "I'm Billy. What's your name?"

"Claire. I'm Claire." Her eyes flicked from me to the pool and back. She had probably never seen death until this morning. One never knows how they'll handle such a thing until it happens. Claire was not handling it well.

"Claire, is there a towel behind the desk I can borrow?"

Claire jumped at the sight of my wet clothes dripping on the floor. I didn't tell her the drops were a mixture of water and blood. She grabbed a towel from a shelf behind her and handed it to me. Her hands were shaking so badly that I was surprised she could hold the towel long enough to give it to me.

"You did a great job, Claire," I said.

Claire didn't reply.

"I heard sirens. Did you get hold of the police?"

She nodded silently.

"That's great. Thank you," I said, trying to boost her confidence.

She nodded again but still didn't say anything.

"How did you find him in the pool?"

Claire's response came out in stutters. "I was sitting here filing inventory lists when I heard a huge splash in the pool. I thought it was someone still partying from earlier, but when I walked out there, the person wasn't moving. I didn't even realize they were dead."

"Did you see anyone else?"

Claire shook her head vigorously. "No."

I turned away from the desk to look out at the pool. From her angle, she could see the pool and the second story on the far side. She couldn't see the middle section or the area above her. "Are there any cameras on the property?" I asked.

"Yes. We have one facing the pool and another facing the entrance."

"But you didn't see anyone enter or exit the lobby?"

"No. No one."

"Is there any other way in and out of the motel?" I asked, a growing alarm ringing in my mind.

"No," Claire answered.

I didn't like her answer, and I didn't say that whoever stuck a sword through Jordan was probably still at the motel. Claire's nerves probably couldn't handle it.

"You said you heard a big splash? Do you think he fell over the railing from the second story?"

"I don't know. It was such a big splash, and it all happened so suddenly. It's like he fell out of the sky."

Claire was already exaggerating the scene in her mind. I might not have been a great investigative journalist, but I knew the chances were slim that a body could fall from the sky into a motel pool. Someone must have pushed Jordan over one of the railings that Claire couldn't see.

"The camera doesn't see past the pool?" I asked.

She shook her head. "It's aimed straight at the pool."

I thought about this for a moment. Claire didn't like the silence. "Are you a cop?" she asked.

"No. I'm just trying to get an idea of what happened."

"You don't think someone else is going to get stabbed, do you?" She looked around to make sure we were the only people in the lobby. Her panic was starting to surface again. The thought of a serial stabber running rampant through the halls was too much for her to handle.

"No one else is going to get stabbed," I said, trying to sound calmer than I felt. "This doesn't look like a random act. Whoever stabbed him did so on purpose and targeted him directly."

"That's good," she responded, but then she caught herself. "I mean, it's sad for him. But it's good for everyone else, you know."

I told her I knew what she meant.

The sound of approaching sirens was growing louder, and Claire and I looked out the lobby windows. Within seconds, a patrol car pulled into the parking lot, and two officers jumped out. They approached the lobby door, scanning the bamboo and cacti for any criminals hiding behind them. They threw open the door and stepped inside, ready for battle. When they saw that it was just us at the desk, their mood eased somewhat. Outside, more police cars flooded into the parking lot with their lights flashing.

"Hello," one of the officers said. "I'm Officer Bennett, and this is Officer Hemphill. Are you the one who called 911?"

Officer Bennett wasn't a tall man, but he held his nose high and walked with his shoulders pulled back. Officer Hemphill was younger than Bennett and had a tense face and anxious eyes.

"Yes," Claire responded. "I called 911."

"What's your name?" Bennett asked.

"My name's Claire."

"Claire, do you believe anyone is still in danger?"

Claire looked at me for reassurance.

Bennett noticed her look. "Who are you?" he snapped.

"My name's Billy. I'm staying here for the night. I don't believe there is any present danger."

"What makes you think so?"

While Bennett asked the questions, the other officers crowded into the lobby and then out to the pool deck. There were so many of them that I wondered if anyone was patrolling the rest of the city. They didn't look nervous or in a hurry. They walked around the pool with their thumbs in their belt loops and glanced up at the guests gathering at the second-floor railing. Officer Hemphill stayed by Bennett's side, still watching for any threat that might attack an entire police force.

"I don't know if it was premeditated," I replied to Bennett's question, "but I'm guessing it was personal."

I told the officers everything I knew, including Jordan's use of the sword the night before and finding him in the pool this morning. I also shared what Claire had told me, and she sat behind her desk, silently nodding in agreement.

Bennett waited to speak again until I had finished. "Well, it's going to be a long morning," he said, running his hand through his graying hair. "We need to talk to each guest who stayed here tonight individually. Claire, do you have a printout or log of all the guests staying here?"

Before Claire could respond, the lobby door opened, and Carter walked in. He was wearing boxers and a white T-shirt. Officer Hemphill moved toward Carter as if he was going to stop him, but Carter brushed past the officer and headed out to the pool deck. A handful of other officers stepped in front of him and raised their hands to signal him to stop, and he did, even though he seemed oblivious to their presence. He simply stared down at the limp figure lying across the deck.

Office Hemphill looked at Bennett, then back at Carter, weighing whether to stay by his boss's side or try to make up for his failed deterrent. He was practically bouncing on his toes.

"That's the victim's father," I told Bennett.

"Wonderful," Bennett grumbled. "Don't go anywhere. I'll be right back."

He told Hemphill to stay in the lobby before walking out to the pool deck. Carter turned his head to acknowledge Bennett, but didn't move from his spot by the pool. Claire and I watched the exchange through the sliding glass doors as if we were watching a silent movie. Carter finally nodded at something Bennett said, took a last look at his son, then floated back through the lobby and up the stairs. If I hadn't met him in the flesh earlier that night, I might have thought he was a ghost haunting the hallways of the Blue Swan.

Bennett waited until Carter had passed through the lobby before coming back in. "Please continue, Claire," he said as he approached the desk. "You said you could print out a guest log, right?"

Claire had to physically shake herself out of the trance induced by Carter's appearance. There were tears on her cheeks for the first time I'd seen. She wiped her eyes, nodded, and turned her attention to the computer to retrieve the requested information.

"Have you contacted your employer yet?" Bennett asked. "We need him here as well."

"I'll call him as soon as this prints," Claire said. She reached for a paper in the printer and handed it to Bennett.

Bennett looked over the paper, then turned to me. "We'll start with you, Mr. Burnes. I know you just told us your story, but if you'll come with us back to your room, I'd like to ask you a few more questions."

Bennett turned to Officer Hemphill, who had now positioned himself directly in front of the door leading to the pool deck. "Hemphill, we need to speak with the guests as quickly as possible. Tell the rest of the boys to knock on every door and talk to everyone. I don't care if they're passed out drunk—wake them up. And don't let anyone leave without my permission."

Hemphill's eyes widened; he nodded frantically as Bennett gave him his orders. Maybe he wasn't good at giving orders to other officers. Maybe this was his first night on patrol. Either way, he was in for an arduous career.

Bennett followed me out of the lobby and up the stairs to the rooms on the second floor. The hallway was lined with people I'd met at the party. Carter was standing at the railing, still in his boxers and shirt, looking toward the pool deck with a vacant expression. Jaselle stood beside him, facing away from the pool deck and silently crying into her hands. Jackie was on the other side of Carter. She looked at me with a helpless expression. I couldn't tell if she had been crying or not. We passed Matt and another guy I didn't recognize from the party; they were leaning in and whispering to each other, but they stopped when we walked by. Leah was standing in the doorway to her room. She had a blanket wrapped around her shoulders, and her gaze was fixed on the ground beneath her feet. Charlie was watching us from the hall across the courtyard. He was gripping the railing with both hands, and I could tell he was panting even from across the open space.

Maybe it was just my imagination, but I felt everyone's eyes on my back as Bennett and I walked down the hallway. Beads of sweat lined my forehead by the time we reached my room. Bennett followed me inside and closed the door.

The night before had been wild, and the morning was bleak. The haze I woke up in was tightening around my spine. It was still dark outside, but I knew I wouldn't get back to sleep anytime soon.

7

I sat at the desk in my room while Officer Bennett paced back and forth across the carpet. If he was trying to be intimidating, it wasn't working. It would have been comical under different circumstances. "You can drop the made-for-TV cop act," I said. "I've already told you everything I know."

"The way I see it is you were the first on the scene," Bennett said, ignoring my snide comment. "That makes you a person of interest."

"Trying to save someone's life makes me a person of interest in their murder?" I asked, probably a bit too sarcastically. I was tired and didn't feel like arguing, but I also didn't want to be pinned down as a suspect.

Bennett blew over my question. "It's also pretty convenient that you were the first person to meet us when we arrived. Maybe you thought that would be a good strategy to manipulate the investigation."

"That probably wouldn't be hard to do," I said, then scolded myself for the brash remark. My brain was working too slowly to stop my tongue.

Bennett furrowed his brow. A touch of frustration crept into his voice. "This is not the time to be smart. We can do this here or down at the station."

"I've already told you everything I know," I said, trying to massage the drum pounding away in my temples. "What's the point of this?"

"Why are you staying here? Are you here alone?"

"Yes, I'm alone, and I'm staying here because I needed a decent place to sleep. That's not a crime."

"Lying to a police officer is," he fired back.

"I haven't lied to you about anything. Please, just tell me what you want so we can get this over with. It feels like I've been up for a week, I just pulled a dead man out of a pool, and now I'd really like to get some sleep."

"Did you recognize the sword in the victim's back before you jumped into the pool?"

"Yes."

"But you still jumped in to save him?"

"Is that a crime?"

"Tampering with evidence is," Bennet scolded. "If you recognized the sword in his back and saw that he wasn't moving, then why did you jump in and try to save him?" He made little quotation mark signs with his fingers when he said "try."

I shrugged. "I don't know. Instinct, maybe? I hope someone would do the same for me if I were floating face down in a pool."

"Well, aren't you a little superhero?" Bennett mocked. "But, from my experience, nobody acts like a hero without some sort of angle."

"That's a sad thing to hear, especially coming from a cop."

Bennett's eyes flared. His voice was strained, like he was struggling to hold back an outburst. "For all we know, you could have jumped in that pool to wipe away your prints or to have an explanation for why your prints would be on the murder weapon."

"Well then, I guess you'll just have to find another way to solve the murder. I'd start with the people he works with. Some of them don't seem too fond of him."

"Listen," Bennet barked. "That's not how this works. I ask the questions. You answer them. People get the crazy idea that they can play cop because they watch a few amateur sleuth detective shows and think they can solve a crime. But they can't. People like *you* need to tell *us* what you know so we can do *our* job."

"People like me?" I mimicked. "What does that even mean?"

Before he could respond, the door opened, and a woman leaned into the room. She had bright red hair and was wearing a black jacket and a detective badge. She quickly scanned the room and then waved Bennett over. They bent their heads together, and the woman whispered something in Bennett's ear while keeping her eyes fixed on me. She was only in the room for a minute before she backed out and closed the door.

"That was the big boss, I'm guessing," I said after the door closed.

Bennett wheeled around to face me. "You think you're smart, and that's what will get you busted, eventually."

"Is that a threat?"

"Take it however you want."

"I think you'd better go now. The boss must want you for something important, like actually searching for the murderer."

Bennett glared at me like he wanted to hit me. I returned his stare, not caring what he did at this point. "If we find out you were involved in this murder, you're going away for a very long time," he said. Then he turned back to the door and let himself out.

I exhaled a sigh of relief after he left. Acting like a jackass was exhausting, even when it came naturally. I looked at the clock. It was already 5 a.m. My attempt at rejuvenation had been obliterated by whiskey, bad influences, and death. It was a recipe ripe enough to corrupt even the best of us.

An hour later, I still couldn't fall asleep. It was unsettling to think that Jordan was still sprawled out on the pool deck fifty yards from my bed. I decided to call my editor, a call he had been expecting for the past week, and I had been putting off. Hopefully, he was still asleep, and I could just leave a message.

The independent news magazine that employed me had paid for a story about life at the border. But instead, their funds had paid for a week's worth of binge drinking and couch surfing. I didn't have the story they paid for, and now I might be tangled up in a murder I had nothing to do with but couldn't walk away from. It was a phone call I was not looking forward to.

I grabbed a glass of water, sat down at the desk, and dialed my editor. He answered with the vigor of a possessed man, despite the early hour. "Billy!" he blurted into the phone. "What the hell? You were supposed to give me updates all week."

"I know. Sorry, Steve," I said. "The week didn't go as planned."

"What the fuck does that mean?" he shouted. I could picture his pasty skin turning a deep red the moment he heard my voice on the line. "Were you robbed at gunpoint? Or pistol-whipped by a border patrol agent because you were doped out of your mind?"

"None of that," I said. "It was just a wild week." Experience had taught me that Steve would lose his muster as his shouting wore on, and that it was better just to sit back and let him blow himself out. But history also showed that I had a habit of provoking the bear for my own amusement.

"A wild week?" he hollered. "A wild fucking week?" His voice grew even louder as he repeated himself. "Do you know how many times I tried calling you?"

When I didn't answer his question, he asked again, but with more profanity. I told him my phone was having reception issues.

"Forty fucking times, Billy! I called you forty fucking times. Good thing I know you're a piece of shit, so I knew nothing bad happened, because bad things don't happen to shitty people. Please tell me you got the story at least."

I told him there was no story our readers would care about.

"I fucking knew it! I knew it was a fucking terrible idea to send your drunk ass to the border. How much tequila did you drink?"

I figured he didn't want an answer, so I didn't say anything.

"What the fuck am I supposed to do, Billy? We gave you five hundred dollars a day to get a story, and you gave us nothing."

"Steve, calm down," I said. "Pull yourself together before you burst. Just tell Corbin that I had some issues at the border and leave it at that. Things are crazy down there, anyway. He'll have to believe it."

Corbin was the founder of *The California Independent*, and he made Steve look like a lamb. He started the magazine a decade ago out of sheer journalistic grit and carried it on his back through meager times. He parted with every dollar as if it were his last ticket to a warm meal and a soft bed.

"You frickin' lunatic," Steve said. "Don't tell me to calm down. You know Corbin won't give a rat's ass about your excuses. He's looking for any reason to get rid of you."

"Do you think I should call him? Try to explain things? He knows how it goes. Sometimes, the story just doesn't have teeth."

"Have teeth? What the hell are you talking about? Are you drunk right now?"

"So I shouldn't call him?" I asked again. It was the wrong thing to ask.

"No, you shouldn't call him, you imbecile," Steve howled. "That's a horrible fucking idea, you fucking drunk. You'll get us both fired."

"What should I do, then?" I didn't want to sound like I was begging for my job. After all, the grave of my career had been dug by my own hand. But I didn't want Steve to get buried with me.

"Don't talk to him until I do," Steve answered. "Where are you now? You were supposed to be back yesterday."

"I'm staying at a little motel half an hour north of the border. It was actually a pretty wild night. There was a corporate party with lots of drinking and lots of glam. One of the guys turned up in the pool this morning with a samurai sword stuck through his back."

There was a pause on the other end of the line. Steve was breathing deeply into the phone, but he didn't say anything for a long time. "Steve?" I asked when I couldn't bear it anymore. "Are you still there?"

"Billy, is this a fucking fantasy? How much did you drink?"

"It's all true, Steve. I found the body floating face down in the pool this morning. I pulled him out with my own hands. And with the help of someone else's hands, technically. But I was the one to jump in the pool and drag him out. The place has been crawling with police ever since. They've had me tied to the interrogation chair for the past hour."

Steve took a deep, exaggerated breath. "You said he had a samurai sword in his back?"

"Yep, all the way through, actually. The handle was sticking a foot out of his back, and the sharp end was sticking a foot out of his stomach."

"Jesus. Did the police find who did it?"

"Nope. We figured it had to be someone who stayed here last night. But there doesn't seem to be camera footage or witnesses to the murder."

I told him the rest of the details. When I finished, he took another deep breath and let the air flutter out through his lips. "Billy, you need to cover this story."

"What do you mean? There's no story to tell yet. Just a crime scene."

"The crime scene makes the story, you moron," Steve replied, as if talking to a child. "A rich kid gets stabbed with an ancient killing weapon and seemingly falls out of the sky. You jump into the pool to save him, but to no avail. That's a good fucking story right there. Hell, it sounds like a goddamn movie script."

"It's not a story. It's a news article."

"Billy, open your fucking booze-locked brain and turn it into a story."

"You're saying you want me to investigate a murder?" I asked skeptically.

"Your frickin' occupational title is investigative journalist." He wasn't quite shouting again, though he was close. "You already talked to the desk clerk and the cops. You took tequila shots with the victim the night before, and then you tried to save him. You might even look like a hero. It's perfect."

"It sounds more like detective work," I said with plenty of apprehension. The idea of searching for someone capable of stabbing another human being with a sword did not sound appealing. "I already went through the interrogation this morning, and they kindly informed me that I'm a person of interest. I don't think they'll appreciate me trying to do their job for them."

"Bullshit," Steve blurted. "Just write what happened and do a little digging into the lives of the main characters."

"I don't know. The whole thing sounds heavy, and it might be over by tomorrow."

"Listen, Billy, you went to the border to write about heavy shit. Corbin paid you a hefty wage to write a story for next month's issue, and you have nothing for him. You know we can't afford to put out another thin magazine, and you know Corbin already thinks you're a waste of space and money. If you come back here with nothing to give him, he might kick you down the stairs before you even set foot inside the office."

Steve wasn't wrong. The writing industry had fired people for less, not to mention wasting the company's hard-earned cash on alcohol and cigars and having nothing but shame and a shriveled liver to show for it. Plus, this wouldn't be the first time I fell short of Corbin's low expectations. He wouldn't just kick me down the stairs; he'd shoot me before I even reached them.

"OK," I conceded. "I'll look into it, but I can't promise anything. Can you buy me some time with Corbin?"

"I'll try," Steve said. "He is going to blow his fucking top, but I'll try to talk him down. How soon can you get me a draft of the party and murder?"

"Let me get an hour of sleep, and I'll get it to you this afternoon."

"Make it early afternoon."

I told him I would. "Thanks, Steve. You're really saving me this time."

"I don't give a damn about you, Billy. If you drag this magazine down, you'll probably drag me down with you, and Melissa won't be happy if I'm not bringing home a paycheck." Melissa was his new bride, whose only passion in life was shopping with someone else's money. The more money Steve made and the less time he spent at home, the happier she was.

I hung up with Steve and laid down on the bed. This time, it felt warm and soft. I dreamed of Jordan laughing like a maniac as his sword sliced through the flesh of fruit flying through the cool ocean air.

8

I woke up a couple of hours later to the sound of someone knocking on my door. I almost yelled at them to go away, but rolled off the bed and opened it. The man in front of me was middle-aged, with a thick handlebar mustache and short, graying hair. He introduced himself as the motel owner and apologized for the inconvenience, but all guests had to vacate the premises. I told him about my assignment to investigate the murder and asked if it would be possible for me to stay. He said all guests were required to leave, per police directive, but he would cover my expenses at the hotel across the street until the Swan reopened.

My first thought was that I would miss the bar at the Swan, even if just for a night. My second concern was that the other guests would follow me across the street. I gathered my belongings and made a weak attempt to tidy up the room. I also grabbed the whiskey shooters from the mini fridge and slipped them into my pocket, assuming the motel staff would be too busy to notice a few missing shooters.

On my way to the lobby, I paused at the hallway railing to get another look at the morning's crime scene. They had taken Jordan's body away, but the red stain still lingered in the pool. A few official-looking detectives and crime scene investigators milled around the pool deck, talking amongst themselves. The red-haired woman detective spotted me watching the scene, and I started walking again. When I looked back over my shoulder, she was still watching me. I left my keycard with the owner at the front desk and told him I'd be back tomorrow.

The hotel across the street looked like it had once been an office building. The receptionist must have seen me crossing the street because she asked why the cops were there. I told her there had been a murder, and her face drained of color. She let me check in early, and I dropped my bag in a guest room the size of an office cubicle before heading out to find a coffee.

The early afternoon sunshine was beautiful despite the gusty winds. The air felt brisk, and the street bustled with life. I was tired but also excited to have a task ahead of me. Like any true professional, I did my best work when my back was against a wall and my gut was full of whiskey, encouraging me to fight back.

I bought a coffee at a little shop down the street and read the local newspaper. Petty crime rates were up in the beach town. Locals blamed the summer tourists for bringing in their evil ways and leaving a trail of disaster on their way out of town. One local retiree called the tourists a swarm of locusts ravaging her way of life. She wanted the hotels torn down, free parking abolished, and the bars stripped of their liquor licenses.

The coffee was good, the shop was cheerful, and both were just what I needed after a disastrous night. The baristas behind the counter leaned in and whispered to each other as they worked. Maybe they knew about the murder from earlier that morning. Maybe they were worried a killer was stalking the streets with a samurai sword and a burlap sack over their head. Or maybe they didn't even care and were discussing their plans for next weekend. It was hard to gather a sense of reality in the fresh air and sunshine.

I pulled out my phone, thinking I should do some research on Jordan before diving headfirst into an investigation. The Carter Real Estate Company had been voted the best small real estate company in the San Diego area for several years in a row. The front page of their website displayed a picture of Carter and the other agents standing shoulder to shoulder on the beach. They were smiling like only the young and wealthy can. The caption below the picture read, "Our dream is to make your dream come true."

The agents page listed each team member along with brief descriptions:

Ross Carter, Owner: Founded the company nearly thirty years ago; continues to work on high-profile deals.

Dustin Rhoads, Senior Agent: Has worked at the company for ten years; voted two-time best real estate agent in the San Diego area; he never loses a deal.

Jordan Carter, Agent: Has worked at the company since he was old enough to walk; has learned from the best in the business; he knows how to help you reach your dream.

Leah Donatelli, Agent: Has been at the company for three years; comes from a long line of entrepreneurs; no one gets better deals than she does.

Charlie Pinkard, Agent: Has worked at the company for three years; he is always available and ready to work for you.

Matt Morris, Agent: Has worked at the company for two years; has experience buying and selling homes nationwide; takes pride in making quick deals for you.

Jackie Alcantar, Office Manager: Has run the office for one year; knows everything there is to know about the industry; if you need anything, ask her.

I typed Jordan's name into the search bar to see which social media accounts popped up. He had a public profile with lots of pictures of him standing in front of big homes with well-dressed homebuyers. There was a girl next to him in some of the photos who was not on the company website. She looked like a model. I wondered if the company had hired her as a marketing scheme.

By the time I finished my coffee and online investigation, it was mid-afternoon. I left the coffee shop and bought a six-pack of beer at a corner store on my way back to the new hotel. A news station had parked its van in the parking lot of the Blue Swan, and a reporter was setting up in front of a camera. I hurried to my room and turned on the TV to the news station matching the number on the side of the van. The reporter was saying that a horrific crime had rocked the night and that the victim's family and friends were devastated. I listened to the reporter ramble on for another minute before changing the channel. Even as a fellow member of the media, I couldn't listen to the story the reporter was spewing. How did she know Jordan's family and friends were devastated? Did she even know that Jordan had been impaled with his own weapon? Amateur reporters like that made my job immensely more difficult.

The weather forecaster on another news station ranted about the high winds and massive swell from the offshore storm. "Tie down your children," he said. "Keep the small dogs inside." The winds would be heavy for a few days, but rest assured, the skies would remain blue, and the sun would shine in all its glory.

I turned off the TV and called Jewels. She said she'd gotten worried when she didn't hear from me last night. I told her about the events from the night before and that I'd need to stick around here for a couple of days to investigate. She sounded skeptical, but then again, I hadn't given her much reason to trust me in the past. We talked for a few more minutes about the case and life at home. A wave of loneliness stabbed me in the heart, but it passed quickly. Jewels told me she loved me and to come home soon.

I typed up a recollection of the events surrounding Jordan's death and sent it to Steve, making sure to leave out the parts about drinking ghastly amounts of whiskey and tequila. Hopefully, the notes were intriguing enough to him and Corbin that they didn't fire me or throw my things out the window. I hit send with a little prayer that they were drinking when they read the email.

After downing the six beers in the confines of the hotel bed, my legs were cramping, and my head felt stuffy. I needed to get outside again. The only decent shirt in my bag was the black polo I'd worn during the party. I laid it on the bed, tried to smooth out the wrinkles, and found a piece of a napkin folded in the pocket of my chest. It had Jackie's name and phone number on it. She must have slipped it in while I wasn't paying attention. I texted the number, asking if anyone would be in the office tomorrow. She responded right away that she would be and told me to come by anytime.

The rest of the day was spent wandering the Point Loma neighborhood with a forty-ounce beer in a brown paper bag. I walked past fishermen, military men, hippies, and bums. Everyone was smiling and happy under the Southern California sun. I passed bars and restaurants where the tables were filled with people eating and drinking the day away. A poster on the side of one of the bars read "Schools, Not Prisons" in big, bold letters. Someone had scratched out the eyes of the man smiling on the poster.

It was dark by the time my wandering led me back to the hotel. The wind had died down, and the air was clean. As I walked, I caught glimpses of downtown across the bay, where the shimmering lights of high rises whispered a promise that wasn't real.

9

The next morning, I went back to the pub down the street for breakfast. I ordered a steak omelet and coffee and asked the bartender if a coffee qualified for a shot at the pony. He said only alcoholic drinks counted, so I told him to put a slug of whiskey in the coffee. He did, and handed me a ball. I missed the shot terribly and returned to my seat, embarrassed by my performance.

When my breakfast arrived, the bartender poured me another coffee and whiskey. I don't know if the coffee made the whiskey taste good, or if the whiskey made the coffee taste good, but the concoction was perfect on a sunny morning. I finished my breakfast and thought about having another round, but decided against it. Then, I drove to the Carter Real Estate Company.

The office was located on the second floor of a two-story building. The ground floor featured a bar and grill with an open patio and lots of sunshine. It looked like a good spot for day drinking. Stairs next to the patio led up to the real estate office. The stairs were wide, slightly curved, and ornate enough for prom photos. I climbed the stairs, thinking that the entire building was designed for sunshine and money.

The Carter Real Estate office was like a massive human aquarium. Every wall was constructed of floor-to-ceiling glass windows, providing the office with a 360-degree view of the ocean and the surrounding neighborhood. It also made everyone inside visible to anyone outside. Jackie was sitting behind the reception desk and waved when she saw me through the windows.

The front door clicked as it was unlocked remotely. I pulled it open and was immediately hit by a wave of artificially cold air. Jackie sat behind a large desk directly in front of the entrance. Behind her was a fish tank big enough for me to swim in, but today it only held dozens of colorful fish. Beyond the fish tank was an open office space filled with desks and armchairs. A banner hung from the ceiling that read "We Make Your Dreams Come True." It was evident that the Carter Real Estate Company only served the privileged and financially lucky members of society.

"Hi, Billy," Jackie said. "You made it." She smiled as she spoke, but her smile looked forced. She was wearing a white silk shirt, her black hair was straight and fell below her shoulders, and her makeup was well done, but I could still see dark circles under her eyes.

"Good morning, Jackie. This is a nice office you have here."

"Looks can be deceiving," she replied quietly.

"Yes, they can be," I said, wondering if her comment was an observation or a warning. "How are you doing this morning?"

"I'm OK," she answered. "I didn't want to come in today, but Mr. Carter said luxury can't afford a day off, and that selling houses gives us the luxurious things we want in this world . . . His words, not mine."

Jackie's desk was neat and well-organized. She had all the essentials a receptionist should have, but there were no pictures of her family or friends, and no personal gadgets that told her to have a great day. I wondered if she enjoyed working here or just enjoyed depositing her paychecks every two weeks.

"How are you, Billy?" she asked. "I feel bad that you got dragged into this whole mess. I feel like it's my fault."

"None of this is your fault," I replied. "You didn't force me into anything. It was my choice to party with you guys."

"Yes, but maybe if I'd just let you have the quiet night you wanted, then you could have avoided us and all our drama. Then you wouldn't have jumped in the pool, the police wouldn't have interrogated you, and you could have just gone home—"

"Jackie," I said, trying to interrupt her downward spiral. "It's really OK. I would have jumped in the pool even if I hadn't met you. And it's going to take more than an early-morning swim to rattle me."

Jackie's eyes were too misty to see that my confidence was a lie. "I wish I could say the same," she said. "I still see Jordan lying on the pool deck whenever my mind wanders. I still see the sword sticking out of him." Her shoulders shook with a slight, involuntary shudder.

"It will pass. Trust me, it always does." I didn't tell her that my solution was usually copious amounts of whiskey. That was no advice to give a sensible person.

Jackie nodded her head, but I knew she didn't believe it.

"Did Carter order anyone else to work today?" I asked, trying to steer the conversation to a more productive topic. A few people were sitting at desks behind the reception area. Some of their faces looked familiar from the night of the party.

"People have been in and out all morning," Jackie answered. "Some had houses to show. It's a little quieter than usual, but honestly, it's business as usual."

"Has Carter been in?"

"I haven't seen him this morning, but I think he was here yesterday because he texted me about a few properties."

I felt my eyebrows climb my forehead. "Working on the day your son was murdered? That's rough."

Jackie nodded. "He's a workaholic; he always has been. It's probably how he's coping."

I looked around again at the faces staring at laptops. None of them had approached me with a sales pitch. They must have already pegged me as an apartment sort of guy.

"Jackie, my editor at the magazine wants me to look into Jordan's death. He basically said my job depends on coming back with a story. I know this puts you in an awkward position, but I'd like to ask some questions around the office, if that's OK?"

Jackie slid a folder across her desk, then moved it back to its original spot. She straightened another folder that was already straight. "I can't promise anyone will talk to you, Billy," she said when she had finished putting her desk back just as it was. "But I might be able to answer your questions."

I had expected more resistance from her. Maybe it was my pretty face, or maybe it was my calm demeanor. But those obviously weren't the case. So I simply said, "That'd be great. Thank you."

"What do you want to know?"

"First off, who was the guy who helped me get Jordan out of the pool?"

"That was Joe," she replied as if that would explain everything.

"Old friend?"

Jackie sighed. "Something like that. He used to work for the company, but he and Jordan got into a fight, and he was let go. He's joined a new real estate firm, but he still holds a grudge against everyone in our office. He pops up now and then to torment us."

"Why was he fighting with Jordan?"

Jackie looked around to make sure no one was sneaking up on us. "I'm not entirely sure of the details," she whispered. "I know that he and Jordan started selling houses around the same time, but that was before I was hired. By the time I got here, they were both accusing each other of stealing the other's listings. Mr. Carter found out and fired Joe."

"They were stealing each other's listings? Meaning Jordan would try to sell Joe's houses, and Joe would try to sell Jordan's?"

"Something like that," Jackie shrugged. "I never got the whole story, and I didn't really know the industry back then."

"Is that sort of thing common in the real estate industry?" I asked. It sounded too cutthroat, even in high-stakes real estate.

"It happens sometimes, but not usually within the same company."

"How long ago was he fired?"

"A little over a year ago."

"Then why was he at the party if Carter fired him a year ago?"

Jackie shook her head. "I don't know. I saw him hanging out by the pool earlier in the night. He's still in the same yacht club as the Carters, and there were other club members there, too. So I thought it had something to do with that, but still, it was weird."

"Definitely odd," I said. "It sounds like he had a motive for revenge, at least, and he was obviously there when it happened, so that's opportunity. But he did seem legitimately surprised that it was Jordan we pulled out of the pool. Either he's a good actor or he really didn't know whose legs he had a hold of."

Jackie shook her head again. "I don't know. We never talked much. He was always kind of sullen and quietly aggressive. You know the type."

I told her I knew the type. "How about around here? Have you noticed anything unusual or anyone acting strangely?"

"You mean acting like a killer?" She said the word killer slowly, as if the word itself would summon a beast armed with a samurai sword. "It's hard to read anyone around here. Sometimes, everyone loves each other and acts like best friends, and other times, they cuss each other out and fight like exes."

"Did anyone cuss out Jordan lately?"

"People don't really badmouth him to his face, being the boss's son and all. But they make their feelings known."

"Fair enough. Has anyone been sharing their feelings lately?"

Jackie paused again. Her eyes narrowed as she bit her lower lip. I wasn't sure if she was trying to remember the past or deciding whether to share it with me. After all, we'd only spent a few drunken hours together, and here I was digging around her office and asking if any of her coworkers had a motive to commit murder.

"You won't report anything I say, right?" she asked hesitantly. "Despite how it might sound, this is a good job for me. It pays all my bills and then some."

I tried my best to reassure her, but my words felt deceptive even as they were coming out of my mouth. "I will do everything possible to leave your name out of it. Anything you know will just help me get started, and who knows if it even leads anywhere. I just need something to point me in a direction."

Jackie glanced cautiously to her sides without turning her head. "OK," she whispered. "I know Dustin was really upset that Jordan got the VP promotion. Dustin has been an agent much longer than Jordan, and, according to Dustin, Mr. Carter made him some promises in the past."

I lowered my voice to match hers. "Promises? Meaning the promotion?"

"That's what I assume. Mr. Carter called the office the other day and asked me to tell Jordan about the promotion. I told Mr. Carter that it made me uncomfortable, but he said he didn't have time to make the announcement. So I sent out a company-wide email informing the agents of the news. Dustin was here when he read the email."

"And he didn't take the news well, I'm guessing?"

"No, he did not. He made a pretty big scene and stormed out," she continued whispering, as if she was worried Dustin might hear and cause another big scene.

"I found a picture of him on your company website, and I remember seeing him with Matt after the cops showed up. But I don't remember seeing him at the party."

"I think he showed up after you left. Originally, he said he was going to spend the night with his family, but then he showed up really late and really wasted. But we were all drunk, so I didn't think much of it." She leaned forward in her chair. "He's here now, too."

I scanned the office space behind her for someone who resembled the agent in the picture I found online. "Is that him by the windows?"

"Yes. Middle desk by the windows.

It was definitely the same guy Matt was talking to on the morning of Jordan's murder. In the few seconds I watched him, he typed something on his phone, set it down, pulled out another phone from his pocket, typed on it, and then slid it back into his pocket before returning to his laptop. Clearly the hyper type, he and I would be mortal enemies at the bar.

"Do you think I could talk to him?" I asked.

"It would probably be best for me to go ask," Jackie said. "We don't usually let people walk in without an appointment."

She spun out of her chair and walked to Dustin's desk. As she spoke, Dustin eyed me from across the office. He seemed skilled at sizing up a man's wallet from a distance, like a twisted version of love at first sight. He eventually nodded, and Jackie returned to her desk.

"He didn't want to talk to you at first," she said as she turned her chair back toward me, "but I convinced him you weren't with the police, and that you only wanted to gather some basic information."

"That was quick thinking. Thank you, Jackie."

She smiled at me. "I hope you find something, Billy. It really freaks me out that someone in this office could be the killer."

I didn't remind her that her desk faced away from everyone else and that someone had stabbed Jordan in the back. I returned her smile instead and walked around her desk to the office space. The panoramic windows offered full views of the beaches below. Tourists and hippies packed the bike path and sand, and surfers bobbed up and down in the ocean's swell. I imagined that if you looked out those windows long enough, you would see every sort of person from every walk of life. This was the edge of the American Dream, and the Carter Real Estate Company was here to sell the dream to the wealthy.

Up close, Dustin was bigger and older than I remembered. His white dress shirt was unbuttoned to the chest and tight enough to show off years spent in the gym. His head was bald and polished. He didn't stand when he shook my hand. Maybe he wasn't impressed, or maybe he just didn't care about manners.

"Hello, Dustin. I'm Billy."

"I know who you are," he said before I could explain myself further. "Jackie said you're a reporter. But the thing is, I have nothing to report." There was an edge to his voice, but his face showed no emotion. His professional mask was well-crafted and practiced.

"I'm not actually a reporter; I'm a journalist. And I'm just looking more into the circumstances surrounding Jordan's death, starting with who he was before he had a sword sticking out of his back."

Dustin's eye twitched, but the rest of his face remained blank. "Unfortunately, I don't know any details about the circumstances of Jordan's passing. I told the cops everything I know yesterday, and I'm not going to tell a reporter anything different."

I resisted the urge to tell him again that I was a journalist, not a reporter. "I don't think we met at the party. You might have come after I called it a night. But then again, someone kept shoving a drink in my hand. I wasn't even planning on drinking that night, but I have this rule about not turning down free drinks, and I lost track of how much tequila and whiskey I mixed."

I felt myself rambling, trying to break down his walls and build a connection. I probably wouldn't get another chance to talk to him if he clammed up now and told me to get lost. Luckily, he had his own questions to keep the conversation going. "Actually, let me ask you something, Billy," he said, leaning forward and glaring. "Why did you feel the need to talk to *me* specifically? Why come here today to my desk?"

Had I been a real detective, experienced in the art of inter-rogation, I might have eased the tension before springing the trap, but instead, my words spilled out without forethought or filter. "Well, Jordan's death wasn't accidental. And seeing as how a lot of people who work in this office were at the scene of his death, there might be some connection between his work and his death."

Dustin wasn't shaken by the faceless accusation of guilt. "Yes, that's obvious. Anyone can see the connection. But why talk to me? Why not talk to anyone else in the office?"

This wasn't going well. I was used to talking with people about their lives and actions, but most of the time, they were willing participants. Interrogation without leverage wasn't my strong suit. To hell with it, I thought. I might as well lay all the cards on the table. "Were you upset that Jordan received a promotion that should have been yours?"

"Who told you that?" Dustin demanded. A flash of rage contorted his face, like someone had squeezed Mr. Potato Head in their hands.

"People talk when they're intoxicated. I listen."

Dustin's eye twitched again. He scanned the office, searching for the company rat. His eyes were stern and calculating as they locked onto me again. "Is this going to be part of your cheap story?"

"Cheap stories have cheap explanations. If I only have one side of the story, then that's all I can write about."

He raised a hand to stop me. "Fine. The answer is yes. Yes, I was upset that Carter picked his son for the VP position. But I won't let that ruin what I have built here. I'm the best agent in this office. Hell, I'm the best agent in San Diego. I've bought and sold some of the most expensive houses in the city, and I don't need an in-house promotion to continue doing so."

"Did Carter promise you the position in the past?"

Dustin's eye twitched. The twitches were coming more frequently as his frustration began to conquer his professionalism. "He never used those exact words," he replied.

"But he implied it, didn't he? He said he would reward you for your loyalty and commitment to the company."

Dustin didn't respond, but his silence and glare answered the question.

"And then he gave the promotion to Jordan without giving you an explanation?" I continued. "That would have upset me if I were in your position."

"Listen. I take my job very seriously." He karate-chopped the air to emphasize how much he cared. "The promotion would have been nice. Very nice. But I can't afford to wallow in emotion. Tears don't sell houses."

"So, you moved on then? And you and Jordan were friendly before he died?"

Dustin cracked his neck and looked around to see if anyone else was listening. Maybe I had pushed him too hard, and a compliment would help ease his testosterone. "It must have taken a lot of patience and professionalism to deal with the situation," I said. "You're a bigger man than I am."

"Don't give me your cheap compliments," he said. "They won't work."

"Got it," I said, then waited a moment before continuing. "Will you answer the question then? Did you and Jordan get along after the promotion?"

"Jordan and I never got along. As I mentioned, I take my job very seriously and hold myself to a high standard. But Jordan's style was different. He was more loose about the job."

"Loose? Like he didn't care?"

"He cared, but he didn't have to work to get here. I, on the other hand, had to spend years grinding and building my reputation. But we still shared the same end goals."

"Like a promotion?" I goaded. "Which you didn't get?"

My words ruffled his composure once again. He leaned back in the chair and clasped his fingers on the desk. He took a deep breath and exhaled slowly. "It looks to me like you're a cheap reporter digging for a cheap story, and I'm not going to play along anymore. So, if there is nothing else I can do for you, then we have reached a natural conclusion."

"One more question. Do you know anyone else who had an issue with Jordan?"

I hoped that the urge to cast the spotlight on someone else would re-ignite the conversation, but Dustin didn't take the bait. "Professionalism," he said dramatically, "means keeping your mouth shut about things that don't concern you. But maybe cheap reporters don't understand professionalism."

I stood in front of his desk for a few more awkward seconds, waiting to see if he would say anything else, but it was obvious he was done talking. "OK, thank you for your time, Dustin." I put my business card on the edge of his desk, as far away from him as physically possible. "My number is on the card if you think of anything else."

He did not wish me a farewell as I walked away.

10

"Billy, one minute," someone yelled before I reached Jackie's desk on my way out of the office. I turned around and recognized Charlie hurrying toward me. He was wearing a blazer that must have restricted his arm movement, and he had tucked a striped collared shirt tightly into dress pants that were too small.

"Hey, Billy. Do you have a minute?" he whispered as he reached me.

"Sure. Where do you want to talk?"

He looked around for a place to hide, but the open floor plan and glass walls offered little shelter from prying eyes or potential killers. "Can I walk you to your car?" he finally asked.

"OK. I'm parked down the street."

Before we left, I asked Jackie for Leah's contact information, and she handed me Leah's business card. I also asked for Jordan's home address. To my surprise, she tore a piece of paper from the notepad on her desk and wrote down the address from memory. The address was somewhere in Pacific Beach. I thanked her and said goodbye. She smiled and told me to call her anytime.

Charlie didn't speak until we were outside. His desperation jumped on me the moment the front door closed behind us.

"I heard you say you were looking more into Jordan's death. Have you found anything? Do you know who did it?"

I started walking down the stairs before answering, also wanting to escape the wall of windows and the eyes behind them.

Charlie followed me but lacked the patience to calm his own nerves. "Come on, Billy. You're not going to talk to me?" He grabbed my elbow from behind. I stopped and looked down at his hand before he took it away. "Sorry," he stammered. "I'm just a little freaked out still."

I continued down the stairs, weighing my options for how to approach this conversation. Charlie either knew something or felt guilty about something. His desperation was pitiful, but his information might be helpful. I waited until we reached the bottom of the stairs before speaking. "Charlie, take a breath so we can talk."

"Billy, I'm fine. I just want to know if you've found any-thing." He spoke in gasps, as if he were trying to get whole sentences out at once. A strong gust of wind ruffled his parted hair, and he frantically tried to comb it back in place with his fingers.

"I haven't found much yet. This is my first stop this morn-ing."

"I saw you talking with Dustin. Did he say anything? You know he's been out to get Jordan for a long time, right? He has to be involved."

It was a heavy accusation given out brashly, especially about someone he shared time and space with. It also seemed a bit suspicious.

"Dustin did admit that he and Jordan went about their business differently," I replied. "But he also said that he'd moved on from the promotion because wallowing wouldn't help him sell houses."

Charlie snorted and put his hands on his hips. "You can't believe Dustin. He would have done anything for that VP position. He wanted it from the beginning, and when Mr. Carter gave it to Jordan, Dustin lost his cool."

"How'd he lose his cool?"

Charlie looked up at the office windows to check if we were being watched. He must not have seen anyone because he continued talking. "Dustin cussed up a storm, saying it wasn't right, and then stormed out. He said something like he brought Jordan into the business, and that he will always be the man in charge."

"What does that mean? Was he some sort of mentor for Jordan?"

Charlie shook his head before I finished the question. "No way. He was definitely not mentoring Jordan. They were always butting heads."

"So what did he mean about bringing Jordan into the business?"

Charlie shrugged and held his shoulders up by his ears for a few seconds. "I don't know."

"Did Dustin lose out on a payday when Carter promoted Jordan to VP?"

"I don't know. Probably. The promotion meant that Jordan would get first choice of property listings."

"How does that work? Listings aren't distributed evenly among agents?"

"They're supposed to. But when a client first contacts the company, Jackie screens them for basic information. If they're a buyer, she asks their desired price range. If they're looking to sell, she gathers details about the house and property. She gives that information to Jordan, who then decides whether to represent the client or pass them on to another agent."

"So Jordan can essentially screen every client represented by the Carter Real Estate Company and decide if the price is high enough for him to take the deal?" It sounded like a great opportunity for Jordan and a bad one for the other agents.

Charlie nodded. "Essentially, yes. There are exceptions, like if we personally recruit a client, but any unclaimed clients go through Jordan first."

"Did Jordan flaunt his new status in front of Dustin?"

"No. Not that I saw," Charlie replied, trying again to comb his hair down against a gust of wind.

"Did Jordan plan to cut Dustin out of big listings?"

"I don't know. I don't think so."

"Did anyone else have an issue with Jordan getting the promotion?"

"I don't know," Charlie repeated. "No one said anything to me about it." He looked down at the ground and kicked an invisible pebble on the sidewalk. Then he started shuffling his feet like he was raking a Zen Garden with the tips of his shoes.

"Is there anything else you can tell me, Charlie?" This conversation was becoming frustrating. My skin itched when I was frustrated.

Charlie looked around nervously at the people passing by on the street. "Me? Nothing. That's why I came to you. All I know is that someone murdered Jordan. Someone stabbed him in the back, and now it's freaking me out thinking that I may work with a murderer."

Charlie was losing his resolve. I silently cursed Steve for putting me in this mess. I could have been relaxing on a patio, sipping whiskey or something fancy like a Mai Tai, and watching surfers tumble into the waves. Instead, I was stuck talking to this fool and making a poor effort at playing detective. "That's why we need to find his killer," I said. "No one should have to live with the fear that they could be the next victim of a serial stabber."

Charlie's eyes widened; he looked down at his stomach, maybe imagining a foot of cold steel protruding from his guts.

"So help me find Jordan's murderer," I said when Charlie's fear had reached its peak.

Charlie gulped and nodded his head.

"What makes you think the murderer is someone you work with?" I asked.

"Doesn't it have to be? We were all at the party together, everyone was drinking, and Jordan had a way of pissing everyone off."

"Did he piss anyone off at the party?"

"I don't remember," Charlie said. "We were drinking so much. Jordan was always loud and getting into people's business. It was hard to tell when he pushed people past their limit."

"I remember you tossing fruit to him. Did he push you past your limit?"

"I admit that was a mistake," Charlie muttered. "Jordan was always trying to make me do things for him that I didn't want to do. He wouldn't stop until I went along with his plans. So I just thought it would be better to do it and get it over with."

"Did he try to get you to do anything else that night?"

Charlie pretended to think for a second. "No. But there was something he said that made me suspicious." His eyes flicked to the sides and up to the office windows. I could tell this was the crux of his desperation, but I wasn't sure if his act was genuine or if he was trying to steer me in a particular direction.

Charlie leaned toward me when he spoke again. "We were sitting by the pool after the whole thing with the sword, and Jordan said that he and his brother had a plan to make a lot of money. And the plan was possible now because of his promotion."

His statement made me pause. There was a lot to unpack in such a brief statement. "I didn't realize Jordan had a brother," I said.

"Well, it's a half-brother," Charlie explained. "Mr. Carter got another woman pregnant at the same time Jordan's mom was pregnant with Jordan. Don't ask Mr. Carter about it, though. He tries to pretend that the affair and his other son, Dereon, aren't real. From what I've heard, Mr. Carter sent them a check every month until Dereon turned eighteen, and that's the only communication he's ever had with them."

"Did Dereon and Jordan communicate often?"

"Not that I know of. At least, not until recently. Jordan never mentioned his brother until he said he was going to meet Dereon at the bar."

"When was this?"

"A few weeks ago, I didn't think much of it until the other night when Jordan said they had a plan."

"Any idea what the plan was?"

"No," Charlie said, shaking his head. "I asked Jordan what it was, but he said I'd have to wait and see."

The secret plan intrigued me. There were only a few things more profitable than real estate in sunny Southern California, and most of them came with jail time. "Do you know how I can get in touch with Dereon?"

Charlie made another feeble attempt at combing his hair. The wind was wreaking havoc on his appearance and fragile self-esteem. "You know what?" he stammered. "Maybe I shouldn't have said anything. I mean, there's probably nothing to it, and I'm probably just acting paranoid. Jordan always told me that I'm too uptight. Maybe he was right."

"Charlie," I said firmly enough to distract the man from his downward spiral. "How can I get in touch with Dereon? Maybe if we figure out what they had planned, then we can understand how it connects to Jordan's murder."

Charlie gulped again. I felt like flicking his Adam's apple every time he did. "Do you think they're connected?" he asked.

"They might be, but we won't know unless you tell me how to find Dereon."

Charlie looked around the street for the hundredth time. When his eyes returned to me, there was a renewed fear behind them. "You won't tell him I told you this, will you?"

"Of course not."

"And you don't think he'll know it was me?"

"I can't answer that for sure. But, Charlie, you might be the only one who can help solve this murder."

"OK," Charlie sighed after another pause. "Jordan said he was going to meet Dereon at the Spark Club. Maybe you can find him there, but remember, you said you wouldn't mention my name."

I thanked Charlie for the tip and left him standing on the sidewalk. He still hadn't moved by the time I got in my jeep and pulled away from the curb. I could see him in my rearview mirror, standing on the street corner like a lost child in this big, scary world.

11

The Spark Club was easy enough to find online. It looked like a rough, gritty place to drink, probably a spot I wouldn't mind frequenting myself. I figured my best chance of finding Dereon there would be in the evening, but it was still only noon. I called Steve to give him an update, and while he wasn't thrilled about investigating at another bar, he agreed it was a worthwhile lead.

I called the number on Leah's business card and left a message. She texted back a few minutes later, saying she was showing a house in Pacific Beach and would be available to meet in a few hours. My stomach growled at the thought of waiting that long, and the coffee-whiskey concoction from breakfast had worn off. So I ordered a burrito and a beer at a 24-hour Mexican restaurant and watched the hippies and early drinkers float through their day. I was a little jealous of the freedom they possessed to drift through life without a care in the world. But then I looked down at my beer, remembered they were hippies, and my jealousy blew away in the wind.

I drove to Pacific Beach and cruised around the neighborhood to get a feel for the area before heading to Jordan's condo. The hippies I'd been watching were replaced by guys wearing tank tops to showcase their bulging biceps and angled traps. I wondered what young, attractive people did for a living that allowed them to walk the streets in tank tops on a Monday afternoon. They must live a blessed life. The only things I'd been blessed with were a sarcastic attitude and a frowned-upon drinking habit.

Jordan's condo was a three-story shotgun house squeezed between two identical condos. The second and third floors had spacious patios and large windows, but all the blinds were closed. A patrol car was parked on the street in front of the condo.

I drove past the police car and parked on the other side of the street. The authorities must have sent someone to watch the property and keep out unwanted visitors while investigators searched for evidence. I hadn't been there long when a white maintenance van pulled up and stopped beside the patrol car. The driver's side window of the patrol car rolled down, and the officer turned to talk to the occupants in the van. After a minute, the police officer rolled up the window, and the van slowly drove away and disappeared around the corner.

A few minutes later, a blue Bronco with a lift kit and over-sized tires pulled up next to the police car. I thought I recognized Matt in the driver's seat, but it was hard to tell from my vantage point. The Bronco idled beside the patrol car as the officer rolled down his window again. Then the window rolled back up, and the Bronco drove off.

Jordan's condo seemed to be a hotspot for activity, especially since he wasn't available to entertain guests. I half-expected Dustin and Charlie to arrive next, but no other vehicles showed up while I waited for Leah to text me back. She eventually did, telling me to meet her at a beachside coffee shop called La Luna. I made a U-turn and turned onto the street where the van and Bronco had gone. The white maintenance van was parked less than a block away. I tried to peek into the cab as I drove by, but the seats were reclined, and I couldn't make out any defining features of the occupants.

When I arrived at the coffee shop, Leah already had a coffee in front of her and was working on her laptop. She was wearing a business suit, but it was low-cut and revealing in all the strategic places. She barely looked up when I sat down across from her at the table.

"Hi, Leah," I said, trying to sound polite and cheerful. "Thank you for taking the time to meet with me."

Leah didn't look up from her computer. "Hi, Billy. I'm very busy. Do you mind if I work while we talk?" Her words were phrased as a question, but her fingers continued tapping away at the keyboard without waiting for a response.

"Sure. No problem. Houses don't sell themselves, right?"

My wit didn't land. Leah continued typing.

"Have you worked at the Carter Real Estate Company for long?" I asked.

"For a few years," she answered, still not looking up from her computer.

"It seems like a profitable place to work."

"It can be."

I took a moment to look around the coffee shop. It was one of those places where everyone added six things to their drink and had all day to drink it. A man and woman were holding up the line as they studied the chalkboard above the register. They were wearing workout clothes, but I couldn't tell if they were heading to the gym or just coming back from it. I assumed their workout attire was more expensive than a night of binge drinking at a downtown bar.

When I looked back at Leah, she was still frenziedly typing away. "It surprised me to see the office open today," I said. "Do all the agents stay this busy with their listings?"

"Some more than others," she replied in a monotone.

Our conversation was not off to a great start. With her appearance, demeanor, and business contacts, she was well-suited to sell mansions to wealthy men. But I wasn't wealthy or in the market for a mansion, so I was of little importance to her.

"How did Jordan get along with everyone in the office?" I asked.

"He had his good days and bad days," she replied. "But I'm sure you already knew that."

"Know what?" I asked a bit too curtly.

Leah paused her typing and looked at me over the top of the laptop. I didn't remember her wearing glasses at the party, but she was wearing them now. They made her look more sophisticated without making her seem older. I wondered if they were real. "Know that Jordan had a tendency to aggravate those around him," she said.

"Did he aggravate you?"

"You are starting to aggravate me with all these questions, Billy." She looked at me as if I were a troublesome child. Maybe in a different life, if she were old and ugly, she would have been a mean elementary school teacher that all the kids were afraid of.

"Yeah, sorry, I have a tendency to do that. What I want to know is why everyone seems to have a similar opinion of Jordan, yet no one ever voiced their opinion directly to him."

"How could we?" she asked. "We work for his father."

"So you just sat there and let Jordan do as he pleased? It sounds like he could make the office a difficult place to work."

"I'm sorry, Billy. Is this an interrogation?" she said, no longer even trying to hide her annoyance. "Because I don't have time to answer these kinds of questions from you."

"No, of course not," I said. "I'm just trying to get the complete picture of Jordan's habits and attitude toward the people in his life."

Leah squinted at me from behind her glasses. They must not have been real glasses. "The answer is yes, Jordan could stir up the office, but I learned how to handle him a long time ago." She looked back down at her computer like the matter had been settled.

"May I ask another question?" I asked carefully. "And I hope I'm not overstepping by asking, but was there a history between the two of you?"

Her phone rang before she could answer. Matt's name appeared on the screen, and she silenced it and turned it over. A tremor of irritation ran through her shoulders and down her arms. "What do you mean, was there a history between us?" she asked.

"Did you guys ever spend time together outside of work? Just the two of you?"

"Is that really relevant?"

"Maybe," I shrugged. "He seemed pretty determined to buy you a drink at the party." I remembered Jordan insisting on getting her a drink and Leah brushing off his arm and his ego. I also remembered Matt putting his arm around her waist, and her letting it rest there for a moment.

Her phone rang again. She silenced it without flipping it upright to see who was calling. "The answer is no," she said. "There was never anything between us. Jordan tried to make a pass at me when I first started at the company. But it was innocent stuff. He was a rich kid used to getting his way. I know how to deal with those kinds of men."

That, I believed. "Did it bother Jordan that you rejected him?"

Before she could respond, her phone rang a third time. She silenced it but peeked at the screen. A flicker of annoyance crossed her face, but it vanished quickly, replaced by a cold, conceited expression. "If you have no more questions about my love life, then I really have to be going," she said. She closed her laptop and stood up without waiting for my reply.

"Thank you for your time, Leah," I said, standing up. "Will you call me if you think of anything else?"

"Of course," she lied. "Have a good rest of your day."

She left the table without pushing her chair in. A man entering the coffee shop held the door open for her. The world was her runway; everyone else was just a pitiful spectator hoping she'd notice them in the crowd. It seemed like an exhausting way to live.

I waited for the door to close and for her to walk past the front window, then I hurried outside. She was stepping into a black Audi by the time I reached the sidewalk. I jogged to my jeep and started it as the Audi pulled away from the curb. She weaved through traffic like a drunk race car driver. I had to speed through red and yellow lights just to keep her in sight. She'd either never been pulled over or had successfully talked her way out of every speeding ticket she ever received.

She suddenly whipped the Audi into a parking lot and stopped in front of a lifted blue Bronco parked alone in the middle of the lot. I parked on the street and leaned my seat back so my eyes just peeked over the window seal. Leah sprang out of her car, her hands flailing through the air. She tried to yank open the driver-side door, but it was locked. So she smacked the window, took a few steps back, and waited for the driver to come out. After a few seconds, the door opened, and Matt slowly stepped out of the Bronco.

Leah didn't waste any time once Matt was out of the car. She stepped up to him and pushed him in the chest with both hands. Matt stepped back and looked around to see if anyone was watching. His eyes passed over my jeep without pausing. Leah didn't seem to care. She moved closer and slapped him across the face. Matt raised his hands to defend himself, but Leah didn't attempt to strike him again. She threw her arms around wildly and leaned toward him as if he couldn't hear her yelling. Her tirade persisted for a few more minutes before she stormed back to her car, slammed the door, and peeled out of the parking lot.

Matt remained motionless until Leah was out of sight. Maybe he was stunned, or maybe he was nervous that she'd return if he made any sudden movements. Then he got into the Bronco and drove slowly out of the parking lot. I turned my face away from the window as he passed by in the opposite direction Leah had gone.

I waited for him to merge with the flow of traffic before making a U-turn to follow. His Bronco was a massive beast compared to the other cars on the road, and it was easy to track through traffic. I congratulated myself for trailing two people in a matter of minutes without being detected. Steven would definitely be receiving a phone call regarding my impressive detective skills.

We were back in Ocean Beach when Matt turned into another small parking lot. I continued driving to avoid drawing attention, but I didn't notice that the street light in front of the lot had turned red. A car driving through the intersection laid on its horn, and I slammed on my brakes. The car sped past with a middle finger hanging out the window. I reversed back to the safety of the intersection line and covered my face with my hand. When the light turned green, I peeked through my fingers at the parking lot. Matt and Dustin were staring at me like a couple of barroom brawlers who'd just been cheated in a game of pool. I drove away, scolding myself for being a reckless idiot.

12

It was late afternoon by the time the Blue Swan reopened to the public. The same guy who had checked me in before was sitting behind the desk. His eyes bulged and his knuckles turned white when he saw me walk through the door with a liquor bag full of whiskey shooters and beer. I asked him how his day was going, and he mumbled something back incoherently. I wanted to reassure him there was nothing to worry about, that I was a stand-up, tax-paying citizen, but there was no point; his mind was already made up that I was a heathen sent to scavenge off the good people of his oasis beach town.

I asked for the same room as the night before. He handed me the key and told me to enjoy my stay; I thought I heard him exhale as the lobby door closed behind me. I climbed the stairs to the second floor and paused in the hallway to reimagine the scene of Jordan's murder. There was a blue tarp covering the pool now, and the deck looked like it had been power-washed. A sign next to the pool said it was closed for repairs.

A waitress emerged from the open sliding glass doors, dragging a table behind her. She stopped next to the spot where Jordan's body had been and knelt down to adjust the table legs. Her knee would have been pressed right into Jordan's lifeless chest less than forty-eight hours ago. I half expected her to jump up when she noticed the water and blood on her pants, but she finished the adjustments, disappeared into the bar for a few seconds, and came back with a pair of chairs. She set them on either side of the table and then continued on with her duties. I wondered if this was some sort of sick joke from the universe—that a married couple would happily enjoy a candlelit dinner on the very spot Jordan had been sprawled out with a sword through his gut.

I shook the image from my mind, got settled quickly in my room, and then headed to a small diner down the street. The hostess was an old Mexican woman who told me to sit anywhere I liked. The only other customer in the place was an old man drinking coffee and reading a paperback. He looked comfortable, like he sat there every night by himself, and it made me sad. But then I told myself he was actually a grand-father with lots of grandchildren and a happy home, and this was his quiet time for himself. I felt better after telling myself that.

The hostess came over, said she was also the waitress, and held up a pot of coffee. I waved off the coffee and asked for a beer. She chuckled and said the closest thing they had to beer was really strong coffee. I told her a glass of water and a sandwich would be just fine.

My sandwich arrived a few minutes later, and I ate slow-ly. The sun had set, and the view from the diner's windows steadily disappeared with the fading light. It felt like we were in a different dimension, cut off from time—as if the rest of the world outside those windows would keep moving on, but those of us inside the diner would never change. It was peaceful, and I understood why the old man came here. I could have sat there all night with a beer and a good book.

By the time I finished eating, it was late enough to begin my search for Dereon. I paid the waitress and left a ten-dollar tip on the table. She smiled and told me they were open all night, every night, and to come back soon. I glanced at the old man and wanted to wave to him, but he didn't look up from his book.

The Spark Club was on the opposite side of downtown, and I took the freeway rather than driving through the city. The neighborhood I pulled into wasn't much different from the one in Point Loma, except it was farther from the ocean and wasn't swarming with tourists. The hippies I'd been cursing at for the past few days were replaced by a rougher crowd that patrolled the streets with aggressive swagger. Tattoo shops and liquor stores lined the streets, but whether or not city planners wanted to admit it, there were liquor stores on almost every corner of the beach communities as well.

The bar sat in the corner of its own small parking lot, disconnected from the other storefronts lining the street, as if it had been constructed at the dawn of the city, and everything else grew up around it over time. It was a rectangular brick building with a door at each end and no windows in between. A sign above the roof read "Spark," but that was the only decoration on the cold, bare bricks. It was made to serve alcohol and built to withstand a nuclear war.

I parked in the back of the lot and walked past cigarette and weed smokers, every one of them sizing me up. This wasn't the first time I'd been to a bar like this, where strangers never get the benefit of the doubt, so I made casual eye contact and tried to look unassuming.

Inside, the lights were dim, and the air was musty, but the music was loud, and the laughter was louder. Almost every seat in the establishment had been claimed by someone with a drink in their hand. I grabbed a stool at the end of the bar and ordered a whiskey. The bartender poured me a double shot but charged me for a single.

"Busy night tonight?" I asked.

"Birthday party," he replied and walked away.

I sipped my drink and tried to gauge the situation. I didn't even know what Dereon looked like, and I doubted people would talk freely. Everyone seemed friendly and appeared to be enjoying themselves, but unwarranted questions from a stranger could turn their energy against me.

My first option was the bartender, even though he didn't seem like the talkative type. When he came over to refill my glass, I asked him if he knew a Dereon who frequented the bar. He tilted his chin down and examined me over the rim of his glasses. "There are a couple of Dereons that come here."

"His last name might be Carter. I'm trying to contact him about his brother."

The bartender stopped pouring my drink and put the bottle down on the bar. "Is his brother in some kind of trouble?"

"Not anymore. He's dead."

The bartender showed no outward reaction to the news, but I could sense him assessing my appearance and words for validity. I met his eyes and held his gaze. I must have passed the test because he picked up the whiskey bottle and finished pouring my drink.

"Dereon usually comes in around now. Stick around, and you might see him." That's all he said before walking off to serve the other patrons clamoring up to the bar.

I was almost finished with my second drink when the bartender leaned over the far end of the bar to whisper in a man's ear. They looked at me simultaneously before returning to their conversation. When they finished, the bartender poured the man a drink, but he stared at it without moving. Then, in a burst of energy, he stood up straight, emptied the drink in a single gulp, and slammed the glass back on the bar. He pushed off the bar and made his way through the growing crowd toward me. People clapped him on the back and tried to say hello, but he nudged past them without responding.

"I'm told you've been looking for me?" he asked as he reached my stool. His face might have resembled Jordan's, but it was hard to tell in the dim lighting. He was tall and well-built, with short-cropped hair and a small mustache. He was wearing dark jeans, a black polo, and a thin gold chain. I imagined he looked good wherever he went, but especially so in a place like the Spark Club.

I reached out my hand to him, hoping the gesture was taken as a sign of goodwill. "Dereon?"

"Who's asking?" he answered without answering, but he shook my hand.

"I'm Billy."

"Alright, Billy. Why are you looking for me?"

I scanned the people around us. The guy next to us might have been trying to listen in, but I couldn't tell for sure. Maybe he was just being nosy. Or maybe he knew Dereon and was waiting for his cue to jump in if the conversation went south.

"Do you want to talk here?" I asked. It was a poor choice of words.

"What the fuck does that mean?" Dereon asked, his voice growing more aggressive.

"Sorry," I said quickly. "Bad phrasing. I just meant it's loud in here. Maybe we can find someplace quieter."

Dereon didn't look around or move. He didn't seem to care about the people bustling around him or notice the music and laughter filling the bar. "Right here is perfect," he said.

"Alright then, I'll get straight to the point. As you probably already know, your brother has been murdered."

The scowl on Dereon's face didn't falter. "And?"

"And I figured you would want to know, if you didn't already. I was there when it happened."

His scowl turned into a smirk. "I heard he was dead. Why would I care, though? It's got nothing to do with me."

I felt a tension release in my gut. "But it's your brother."

"Nah. He ain't my brother."

The tension in my gut eased even more. I had hoped that the eighteen years of child support Carter had paid, instead of providing fatherly love, had left a void in Dereon's heart. But from Dereon's reaction, his father's avoidance had stirred up stronger feelings than just indifference.

"I get it," I said. "The first time I met him, he was hammering tequila shots and swinging around a samurai sword. But now I'm trying to find out who might have put that sword through his back."

Dereon's expression shifted once again. "You a cop?"

"No, I'm an investigative journalist."

My assertion that I wasn't with the boys in blue didn't seem to pacify him. "A journalist? You're looking for me so you can write about me?"

"No, not at all," I said, waving my hand as if that would convince him. "I'm trying to figure out if there was anything more to Jordan than the party boy, asshole I met before he ended up face down in a pool. So when I heard he had a brother, I figured I had to meet you."

Dereon was shaking his head before I finished. "Stop calling him my brother. And you're asking the wrong guy. I knew he existed, but that's the extent of our family connection."

"So you weren't close then?"

"Hell no," he answered in a higher pitch. "His dad got my mom pregnant and left us with nothing. His rich-ass lawyers even got him out of paying full child support. I've been scraping by my whole life while they cruise around on their yachts and piss on the rest of us."

"Did Jordan feel the same way as his father?"

"Man, he was the worst one. He rode his daddy's coattails his whole life and never had to do shit for himself."

"I was told he recently contacted you?"

Dereon instantly tensed back up. He looked at me again like I was a snake in the grass. "I don't know what you're talking about," he said.

We had reached a pivotal point in the conversation. I considered standing up from my barstool so we'd be closer to eye level, but I didn't want it to seem like a threat. "I know you weren't there when Jordan was killed," I said. "That's not what I'm here for."

"Then why are you here?"

"I want to know what Jordan had in mind for you."

Dereon paused again. I thought he might walk away, but he didn't. "You got nothing to do with the cops?" he asked.

"Absolutely nothing," I replied.

He was quiet as he thought it over again. The people around us were loud and drunk. Someone was yelling a story by the tables, but I couldn't see them through the mass of people crowding the bar. The story ended, and everyone burst into laughter.

"Listen," I said. "From all accounts, Jordan was not a great guy, and the apple doesn't fall far from the tree. Whatever information you have about Jordan can't hurt him now, but it might have implications for people still breathing."

Something flashed behind Dereon's eyes. Maybe it was a fleeting vision of retribution for a lifetime of neglect. "OK," he said finally. "I'll tell you what I know. But you can't put my name in your investigation, or I'm not saying shit."

"Deal," I said, trying to sound reassuring.

"And it's going to cost you."

"How much?"

"How much cash you got?"

"Not very much."

"How much is not very much?"

I tried to remember how much cash was left in my wallet. I had wasted so much of it drinking the past few days that it was hard to keep track of. "Something like three hundred, but I'd have to check."

"Well, go ahead and check then."

"I'm not going to check right here, if that's what you mean."

"Then you'd best go check somewhere else and let me know."

I slid off the stool and walked past his beaming smile to the bathroom. It was a single-use bathroom, and I waited in line with my head against the wall, feeling like a junkie waiting for my turn to chop something up on the back of the toilet.

"I can give you two hundred and fifty," I told Dereon when I returned to the bar.

Dereon smiled. "I'll take it."

"That's a hefty price for information that might not be helpful."

"Oh, it will be helpful." His smile grew wider. "Trust me."

He headed for the door without looking back, and I was forced to follow. We cut through the growing crowd in the parking lot toward the back corner, where Dereon got into a lime green Chevy Nova. A handful of partiers shouted to

Dereon that he better not be leaving so soon. Dereon waved back and pointed at me. I wasn't sure what the gesture meant.

"Nice ride," I said as I climbed into the passenger seat. "Are we going somewhere?"

Dereon didn't answer right away. He looked at the people laughing and drinking in the parking lot, then at me, then back at the party. "Nah, man, we aren't going anywhere. I just didn't want to talk inside is all."

"What can you tell me? Hopefully, it's worth two hundred and fifty dollars."

"Give me the cash first."

I pulled the cash out of my wallet and handed it to him.

Dereon took the money and put it in his pocket without counting it. "Good," he said. "Now get out."

My breath caught. "You can't be serious."

"Nah, I'm just messing with you, man," Dereon said, laughing at his own joke. "Jordan came to me the other day about some bullshit plan to make some money. I told him I'd think about it because he wasn't taking no for an answer. But I just wanted him to shut the hell up and get out of here."

"What was the plan?"

"Drugs. He said they've been using empty mansions as stash houses. He said it's perfect because no one suspects multi-million-dollar homes, and he is the only one with the keys—"

"Wait," I interrupted. "Jordan has been dealing drugs out of his listings?"

"Nah. Someone brings them over the border, and Jordan hides them until someone else comes to pick them up. Jordan is just a middleman."

It was my turn to look around the parking lot and consider Dereon's words. Although I had suspected something like drugs, it still seemed like a bold move by Jordan. Using his real estate listings as temporary stash houses actually made sense. But the logistics of moving the drugs in and out, along with the foot traffic of potential home buyers, would be problematic.

"He must be making some profit from it," I said.

"Must be," Dereon replied. "Or why else do something that stupid?"

"What did he want from you?"

"He said he was getting ripped off by taking all the risk and not getting paid enough. So he hatched a plan to break down the shipments and sell them himself. He wanted to know if I had any connections that could help him with distribution. But I've never sold a gram of anything in my life. That little prick just assumed I had."

"So you told him no?"

"Hell yeah, I told him no. I've made it this far in life without him and his dad. I didn't intend to get mixed up in any of their shit."

"Did he say his dad was involved?"

Dereon shook his head. "He didn't say. He just said he and some other guys with access to open houses were making good money but had a plan to increase their profits."

"Meaning guys from the Carter Real Estate Company?"

"That's what I assumed."

"Did he say anything else?" I asked. "Like which house they were using or when another shipment was coming?"

"Nah. He kept talking about how much money we could make and how the plan was perfect. But I knew it would never work because that motherfucker couldn't keep his mouth shut. Take me, for example. He didn't really know me. But within five minutes of sitting at this bar, he told me his entire operation."

I obviously didn't know Jordan very well, but I agreed that he was too impulsive to handle an operation that required discretion and composure. Dereon and I were silent for a minute. Neither of us knew how to proceed. I was the one to break the silence. "Dereon, I wasn't sure if you were going to talk to me, but this may really help. Thank you."

"You going to take it to the police?"

"No. I'm going to continue my own investigation."

"Good. I'm no snitch, but I really don't like Jordan or his dad. And seeing as how Jordan is dead, and I had nothing to do with it, I figured it wouldn't hurt to tell. Maybe if you do some more of your investigative journalism, you can bust the rest of them. They deserve it."

"I'll see what I can do. It's an interesting development."

"Come on, man, let's go back to the bar," Dereon said, opening the car door to signal our conversation was over. "There is one more thing you can do for me."

We got out of the car and went back inside. We squeezed up to the bar, and Dereon called the bartender over. "Hey, Herb," he shouted over the music and commotion. "This man here said he'll buy a drink for everyone sitting at the bar."

Herb nodded in acknowledgment without even looking at me for confirmation or protest. He grabbed a handful of shot glasses and walked the length of the bar, placing a glass in front of each patron sitting on a stool. Two women shouted like they'd won the lottery when Herb set glasses in front of them.

"I hope this is coming out of your payment," I said to Dereon's back.

He spun around and gave me his best smile. "Nah, man. This is your way of thanking the bar."

Herb filled the shot glasses in front of Dereon and me, and we downed them. Dereon told Herb to fill them back up, and we finished those, too. I said goodbye and zigzagged through the crowd to the back door. Outside, the night air was crisp, and the moon was full. The drinking had spilled deeper into the parking lot, where people sat on the hoods of their cars with beer bottles and plastic cups. There were no murders or bombs that could stop the party from rolling on at the Spark Club.

13

I woke up the next morning hoping I was lying in a bed at the Blue Swan. I lifted my head off the pillow, recognized the room, and then dropped back down in relief. The memory of driving home from the Spark Club was hazy. I had a vague recollection of trying to find the right exit off the freeway and stopping at a liquor store for a six-pack. I whispered a prayer that my jeep was parked safely and intact in front of the motel.

My phone and keys were sitting on the nightstand next to the bed, usually a good sign after a night of heavy drinking. I grabbed my phone. It was 8:35 a.m. There was a text from Jackie saying Jordan's memorial service was starting at 11 a.m. at the Statesmen Yacht Club. I thanked her and wondered how it would be possible to follow this story without her help.

My body groaned as I sat up, and my brain felt like it had rotted in my skull. I stood under the shower until my skin wrinkled, then called the front desk to ask if someone could bring me a bagel and a cup of coffee. By the time someone knocked on the door, I was dressed and watching the news. I ate the bagel plain, added a whiskey shooter to the coffee, and flipped between news channels. The weather forecasters were still hollering about the wind and ocean swell. "Save the women and children," they cried. "Run for the hills." I pulled aside the window curtain, looked up at a beautiful blue sky, and promptly turned off the news.

I left for the Statesmen Yacht Club at 10 a.m. It was located on the downtown waterfront, a stone's throw from the towering high-rises that dominated the city skyline. The road to the club curled around the edge of the bay, with the airport on the left and the water on the right. A bike path ran alongside the shoreline, and two women were jogging in the fresh Southern California air. They were tan, fit, and could have been filming a commercial.

The sun sparkled off the water of the bay like a field of liquid diamonds. There were so many boats crammed on the docks that it was difficult to pick one out from another. A sailboat passed by, just feet from the shore; its sailors were long-haired, shirtless, and leaning off the boat like raiding barbarians. Further up the road, a retired aircraft carrier stood watch over every vessel passing through. Even further up the road, the Coronado Bridge rose up and away from the city, its blue underside matching the color of the ocean below.

The morning bristled with the feeling that something was about to happen. Something amazing and life-changing was just around the corner if I ran fast enough. I didn't know what it was, but I knew it was coming, and it made everything seem more brilliant in the morning light.

I remembered making plans with my college roommates about getting rich and famous. We were going to start our own business or invest in the next viral company. We knew we would be stars. We knew we would change the world. I felt that way now in the radiant sunshine, and I found myself smiling for no other reason than simply being here and alive.

As the road curved around the bay, the airport disappeared from view, and the high-rise buildings stretched toward the sky. I imagined it would be a hell of a view from the tops of those buildings. Down on the streets, the constant flow of cars and pedestrians pumped life into the heart of the city. A man pushing a shopping cart along the sidewalk warned the office workers and tourists that the devil would devour them all.

The Statesmen Yacht Club was barricaded from the public by a ten-foot wall. The words "San Diego's Most Exclusive Yacht Club" were painted on the wall to mock the general public who couldn't afford the membership dues. The only apparent points of entry were from the ocean or through a security checkpoint. I drove up to the security kiosk and greeted the security guard with my best smile. He was an older man who looked like he had been following orders his entire life.

"Are you a club member?" he asked.

"No," I replied. "I'm here for Jordan Carter's memorial service."

He ignored the mention of a memorial service. "All guests must be accompanied by members," he droned.

"I was invited by one of your members."

"You must be accompanied by them to enter."

This guy was getting on my nerves. He needed a six-pack, a cigarette, and a direct order from his boss to jump in the ocean. "Has Ross Carter or Jackie Alcantar arrived yet?" I asked.

"I cannot tell you that."

I stared at him for a moment. "So there's no way you'll let me in alone?"

"Not a chance."

"Great," I said, then turned my jeep around.

Since there was nowhere to park on the street, I drove to a nearby corner parking lot and paid the all-day fee. As I was walking back to the club, a black SUV pulled up beside me, and the window rolled down. Jaselle was sitting in the passenger seat. "Hi, Billy," she said in her feather-like voice.

"Hello, Jaselle. I'm happy to see you," I said, then realized it wasn't a very polite thing to say before a memorial service.

Carter leaned forward in the driver's seat to look past Jaselle. "Morning, Billy. I didn't know the press was covering my son's memorial."

"I hope I'm not intruding," I said, then scolded myself for making another dumb comment, like intruding on a funeral was the same as walking into the lunchroom unexpectedly. I was not off to a good start.

"I've been told that you're investigating my son's murder," Carter said. His tone was severe enough that Jaselle turned her head to stare blankly out the front windshield.

"Yes, I have. I was hoping to talk to some guests after the service, if it wouldn't be too much trouble."

Carter paused as he considered my proposal. I thought that if the roles were reversed and it was my son who had been murdered, I would have kicked any journalist trying to intrude on his memorial. But Carter eventually nodded and asked if I needed a ride to the club.

"Yes, please," I replied. "The guard at the security kiosk thought I was a danger to the public."

"Jump in," Carter said.

I opened the back door and got in. Jaselle turned around and smiled. "Hello again, Billy," she said pleasantly. "You look nice today." Her lipstick was the same bright red she had worn at Jordan's party. She was wearing a beach hat and a black summer dress over a red bikini top. I thought it was an interesting choice of attire for a memorial.

"Thank you," I said. "You do as well. And thank you for the ride in, although I wish it were under different circumstances."

Carter glanced at me in the rearview mirror. "Me too, Billy. But I'm glad the club is holding a memorial so soon, so we can start moving on."

We pulled up to the security gate, and Carter made quick small talk with the guard, who offered his sympathies for Jordan's passing. The guard waved us through without asking for Carter's membership card. We drove down a short driveway lined with swaying palm trees and perfectly manicured lawns. For being the most exclusive yacht club in San Diego, the Statesmen Yacht Club was not very big or fancy. The driveway ended in a narrow parking lot that stretched from one end of the club to the other. There were a few simple wooden buildings on stilts spaced out between the parking lot and the water. But the yachts docked on the other side of the buildings were spectacular. I figured I'd have to save my paychecks for ten lifetimes to afford one of them.

We parked in front of the largest building, which Carter said was the clubhouse. Two male employees, dressed in baby blue shirts and white shorts, came out to greet us. They were tall, handsome, and looked hand-picked from a magazine. They shook hands with Carter and hugged Jaselle. Carter told them he had bags in the back of the SUV to be loaded onto his boat. They smiled, vigorously shook their heads, and said they would get to it right away. We left them in the parking lot and headed for the clubhouse. As we walked up the stairs, I looked back at the wall that separated the club from the outside world and wondered which side it was meant to protect.

I'd never been inside the clubhouse of a yacht club before, but it resembled any clubhouse at a thousand different golf courses—except the windows looked out to yachts and salt-water instead of golf carts and grass. There was a bar along one wall, booths and tables along the opposite wall, and a large circular fireplace in the center. Jordan's headshot was propped up on an easel in front of the windows, with some flowers and candles around the base. Of course, Jimmy Buffett played through the speakers, telling us all about life in a tropical paradise.

A modest crowd had already arrived and settled into scattered groups. I recognized a few faces—Charlie, Matt, Dustin, and Leah were at the bar with a young blonde woman. Their hands were full of drinks, and their conversation was full of laughter. Jackie was talking to an older woman in front of Jordan's picture. Carter remained in the back of the room with Jaselle, shaking everyone's hand as they arrived. It was the happiest memorial I had ever been to and, consequently, the saddest.

I made my way over to Jackie and the older woman. Jackie was wearing a black tennis skirt and tank top, and I wondered if every beach memorial came with a beach-themed dress code. "Hi, Jackie," I said. "Thank you for the heads-up."

Jackie's face lit up when she saw me. "Hi, Billy! Thanks for coming. I figured you'd want to be here." She motioned to the older woman standing next to her. "This is Nancy, Jordan's mom."

Nancy was a short woman with tired eyes and drooping cheeks. Unlike the other guests, she was not dressed for a day at the beach. She looked out of place among the glamour of the yacht club, and I wondered if Jordan would still be alive if he'd been more like her.

"It's nice to meet you, Nancy. I'm Billy," I said as I reached out my hand to her.

She gave me a strained smile and shook my hand. Her hand was small and frail. "Hi, Billy. Jackie told me you're an investigative journalist."

"Yes, I am. I hope that doesn't give you a preconceived notion about me."

"Why would it?"

"I don't know. But it makes some people raise their guard."

"Are you investigating my son's murder?"

"Yes."

"And you aim to find out who murdered him?"

"Yes."

"Then my guard is down," she said, and for a brief moment, a look of determination replaced the anguish on her face. She was the first person I had met in two days who I think genuinely cared about Jordan. "Have you found any information?" she asked.

Before I could answer, someone burst out laughing from the direction of the bar. Everyone in the room paused their conversations and looked toward the bar for the culprit. The young blonde woman who had been talking with the real estate agents covered her mouth and raised a hand apologetically to the crowd staring at her. Now that I could see part of her face, I recognized her as the girl in the pictures on Jordan's social media page. She was wearing a white sundress and a white bikini underneath.

"Who's that?" I whispered to Jackie.

"That's Kylie," she whispered back. "Jordan's girlfriend."

"I didn't know Jordan had a girlfriend."

"Yep," Jackie whispered. "She's an Instagram model." Her tone suggested I could learn everything there was to know about Kylie's character from her choice of occupation.

"She doesn't seem too distraught," I said.

Jackie shook her head and scrunched her lips. "I don't know if she cares about anyone other than herself."

Kylie turned her back to the crowd and hid her face behind her hands, and the crowd went back to their private conversations. I turned to Nancy, who had also been staring at Kylie. "I'm sorry. You asked if I had found any information?"

"Yes," she replied. "I tried asking Ross, but he didn't have any answers. I tried asking the police, but they wouldn't tell me anything. I feel like I'm the only one who cares about finding out who killed my son." She pulled a tissue out of her pocket and dabbed her eyes. Jackie squeezed her arm reassuringly.

"I may have," I said. "It looks like your son was getting mixed up with an ugly crowd."

Nancy stopped wiping her eyes and squinted at me over the tissue. "What do you mean?"

"I can't say for sure at this point," I answered, making a conscious effort not to look around the room. "But Jordan might have been doing some extra business with the houses he was listing, and he may have upset the pecking order."

"Are you telling me another real estate agent killed my son?" Nancy asked. I could tell it was a question that had already crossed her mind. Jackie didn't flinch at the question either.

"That is a possible scenario. But it might extend beyond just real estate agents—"

"What makes you think that?" Jackie interrupted, her expression tense. Maybe she was worried about getting dragged into the mess, or maybe she already had her own suspicions.

I gave her a quick, apologetic nod. "I'm sorry. I can't explain any more right now. But hopefully this lead pays off, and I'll have more information soon."

Nancy looked at me with appraising eyes, trying to decode the meaning behind my words. I felt sorry for stringing her along. But I wasn't sure if the part about using empty homes as stash houses was true, and I didn't want to complicate her feelings any more if it wasn't necessary.

"I know my son had a tendency to be brash," Nancy said. "Unfortunately, he took after his father. I tried telling him to ease up, but he wouldn't listen."

"I take it he was always ambitious?"

"Oh yes," she answered. "And probably a bit entitled. Jordan thought he was destined to be the biggest agent in the city." It was an honest opinion coming from a mother about her son, and I wondered again how Jordan didn't turn out more like her.

"How long had he worked at the real estate company?" I asked.

"He was in my ex-husband's office since he was a little boy, but they didn't always have the fancy office they have now." She glanced at Jackie, who was listening intently. "Jordan was born shortly after Ross and I moved here from Texas. Ross started the company in an old office building in El Cajon. Are you familiar with El Cajon? It has its rough parts. Anyway, Jordan was in the office the minute he could walk."

"I'm not familiar with El Cajon," I said, "but you don't see many people moving from Texas to California anymore. It's usually the other way around."

Nancy nodded. "Ross and I both grew up on cattle ranches, but Ross didn't want to spend his whole life raising animals, and I wanted to live by the beach. We both dreamed of California."

"So you packed up and left?"

"We hardly had anything to pack."

"And you started a real estate company with a baby in tow?"

"Yes. Ross said that having a baby in the office boosted his credibility with homebuyers. It always made me so mad when he said things like that."

"So Jordan was basically raised in the industry?"

"He was. He grew up with the company and watched his father build the business into what it is today. As Jordan got older, he saw the lifestyle that money could buy, and he wanted that for himself. I tried my best to give him a decent upbringing, but since I didn't see him every day, my influence eventually faded. I was in constant battle against all the things young men desire in life, and I was on the losing side."

It sounded like the same battle waged between most mothers and their sons, except amplified by wealth and prestige. I felt sorry for Nancy and didn't know what to say. "It must have been difficult to raise a child under those circumstances," was the best I could do.

"It definitely was," Nancy said. "When kids are young, all they crave is love and attention. But Ross was too busy to give Jordan either. He was in the office all week and showed houses on weekends. When Jordan couldn't get the love he wanted from his father, he learned to value other things in life. He saw the attention Ross got from building his business and saw the shiny things Ross cared about, and he wanted all of those things too. But Jordan was too young and naive to understand the costs of running a business."

"Including the cost of your marriage?"

Nancy paused for a moment and then nodded. "Yes, including our marriage." She glanced at Carter, who had his arm wrapped around Jaselle's waist. Nancy didn't appear jealous or angry. If she was feeling anything at all, I thought she might be lonely.

"Like I said, Jordan saw the things his father had and wanted them too," she continued, still watching her ex-husband and his young bride. "When Ross and I first split, we shared joint custody of Jordan. But I moved into a small apartment, and Ross kept our home and most of the money. Jordan had already learned to cherish the things that I couldn't give him, so he eventually lived full-time with Ross. I often wonder if there was anything I could have done differently as a mother to keep him with me."

It was a dark thought that must haunt all parents who have lost a child, but it wasn't Nancy's fault that Jordan had chosen his path. From a young age, Jordan had crafted an image of what his life should be like, and from then on, everyone became a tool to achieve his vision. His mother couldn't help him achieve those dreams, so she was cast aside.

I thanked Nancy for talking with me and promised to continue investigating. She thanked me with a sad smile that said she had lost her son a long time ago.

14

Jackie and I went to the bar for a drink. The bartender had just set a shot of whiskey in front of me when Carter tapped Jackie on the shoulder and said it was time to go. He walked away without saying anything more. I looked at Jackie and raised my eyebrows, silently asking why it was already time to leave.

She tilted her head and smiled sheepishly. "Oh, yeah. The actual service is taking place on Catalina Island."

"You failed to mention that in your text this morning," I said.

Jackie hunched her shoulders, her awkward smile intensifying. "Sorry. Mr. Carter told me it was on Catalina after I texted you. I had to scramble to get my things together and forgot to text you back."

"Are we staying for the afternoon?"

Jackie clasped her hands together as if in prayer and held her fingertips up in front of her face. "I think we're staying until tomorrow. I'm so sorry."

I looked around the room and saw a pile of bags near the door. They were probably waiting to be loaded onto a boat that would take us to the island. I looked down at my dress pants and short-sleeved polo and immediately felt very unprepared for the day and night ahead. Jackie must have read my mind. "I'll ask one of the guys if they have an extra jacket," she said.

"That'd be lovely," was all I could say in return.

We grabbed Nancy and went outside to the balcony. The sunlight reflecting off the polished cabins of millionaires' yachts caused the air to shimmer. A gust of wind slapped me in the face as a not-so-pleasant welcome to the adventure ahead. I remembered my jeep parked in the day-use parking lot and told myself I'd ask Carter to cover the tow truck fee. But I knew I wouldn't ask, and that made me feel worse.

The rest of the memorial service was already moving down the docks toward their boats. Club employees trailed behind, carrying overnight bags and ice chests. Jackie told me to follow her, and we joined the parade.

I heard Matt and Dustin before I saw them. They were laughing and strutting down the dock like they were filming the intro to a reality TV show. Leah was with them. They caught up and passed us on the narrow dock. I think they would've knocked me into the water if I hadn't stepped aside.

"Well, look what the cat dragged in," Dustin said as they sauntered by. "You just don't know how to stay away, do you?"

I wanted to fire something clever back, but couldn't think of anything good to say. "How could I turn down a trip to Catalina?"

"Careful out there on the island, Billy," Dustin teased. "There are a lot of things that like to bite." Matt and Leah laughed like Dustin had said the funniest thing in the world.

"Hey, Carter," Matt said, imitating a shout over his shoulder. "We've seen how this guy drives. Don't let him get behind the wheel." They laughed again and skipped down the dock.

"Animals," Nancy scoffed.

"Don't worry about them," Jackie said, trying ineffectively to offer encouragement. "They just like to talk, but they're harmless."

"Are you sure about that?" I asked.

"Yes, don't worry. Nothing is going to bite you on the island," she chuckled, but it sounded fake. I looked back toward the clubhouse and wondered if I could sneak away without anyone noticing, but Jackie started down the dock again, and I was forced to follow.

Carter's yacht wasn't the biggest on the dock, but it dwarfed any boat I had ever been on. The name "Lynn Dixie" was painted on the side in blue letters. I climbed aboard and found a spot to stand in the far corner of the deck. The other passengers took seats inside the cabin. Carter was the last to board. He hopped on with an energy that was surprising for an old man in mourning. He started the engine, finished his pre-launch routines, and before long, we joined a caravan of yachts pulling away from the yacht club.

The offshore storm that the weather forecasters had been raving about hit us full force as soon as we reached open ocean. Driving winds and pounding waves beat us back as if Mother Nature was warning us to return to the safety of the bay. The other passengers remained huddled inside the cabin where they could avoid the elements. I had been on these waters before as a kid and remembered being fascinated by a pod of dolphins that danced and raced through the water. Now, I strained to see any signs of life above the whitecaps and rough ocean swell.

At one point, Jackie stepped out of the cabin holding a red Solo Cup in one hand and a jacket in the other. "What's this?" I asked when she handed me the cup.

"I don't know. Mr. Carter poured it and told me to bring it out to you."

It smelled like rum. I emptied the cup and coughed hard. It was definitely rum.

"You can come inside, you know," Jackie said, taking the cup back from me and handing me the jacket. "This is also from Mr. Carter."

I thanked her, put on the jacket, and waited for her to say something more. "I'm really glad you're here, Billy," she said and smiled. Then she turned, grabbed hold of the railing, and slowly made her way back to the safety of the cabin.

I watched her go and realized Carter had been watching us from his spot at the helm. He raised his cup in the air, and I waved to him. Then he turned back to the steering wheel, and I turned back to the wake carved by the yacht in the turbulent ocean waves.

We reached Catalina Island after a couple of hours of slow slogging. We hit the southern tip of the island and headed north along the inside coast. We sailed past barren coastlines and beaches filled with seals. We sailed past the city of Avalon, with its distinctive Grecian theater seemingly built right on top of the water. The rest of the picturesque town climbed up the hillside like a city from another country and another time. We sailed past Two Harbors and the ferry carrying families from the mainland. We kept sailing north until we arrived at a small bay at the far tip of the island.

Jaselle emerged from the cabin, wrapped in a blanket and looking pale. She shuffled to the edge of the boat, and for a moment, I thought she might fall over the side. But she steadied herself and stood still, taking deep breaths and watching the island. The wind blew her blonde hair across her face, but she didn't try to stop it.

Dustin and Matt came out to the deck with Solo Cups in their hands and grins on their faces. They heaved an inflatable dinghy overboard and loaded it with ice chests and overnight bags. Carter climbed into the dinghy, and the three of them headed for shore. When they reached land, they quickly unloaded the dinghy, and Carter pushed it back into the water and returned to the Lynn Dixie.

When it was my turn to ride, I climbed in and helped Jackie and Nancy into the dinghy. Carter handed me Jordan's memorial picture and the easel. I reached for them without thinking, but hesitated when I realized what they were. Carter didn't seem to notice or care. He shoved them into my hands and jumped into the dinghy. I set the picture in my lap and covered it with a beach towel to keep it dry. I also preferred not to have Jordan's frozen smile staring up at me. It was eerily similar to the morning I sat next to his lifeless body—except he hadn't been smiling then.

When we reached the sand, I got out and offered Nancy a hand again. She nearly pulled me into the water as she stepped out of the dinghy. Then she stormed up the beach, cursing the ocean and the ever-churning waves. The beach we had landed on was a mix of soft sand and jagged pebbles. It would never make the cover of a travel magazine, but its ruggedness and distance from the tourist spots gave it a feeling of isolation. I assumed the club members usually found the seclusion appealing, but now it meant there was nowhere to run if someone pulled out a machete and decided to start hacking.

We walked along the beach past colorful kayaks and concrete fire pits to a large mess hall. It had big windows and a wrap-around porch. Behind the mess hall, there were rows of smaller cabins and enough palm trees that vacationers could squint and imagine they were in the tropics.

Matt and Dustin were drinking beers and smoking cigarettes on the porch. They laughed when they saw me trudging through the sand. "Not much of an island type, are you, Billy?" Matt said with a wide grin. He was always grinning, and it made me want to slap him. He was also wearing those damn yellow-tinted glasses that made him look like a sick cat, and I had to fight the urge to slap them off, too.

"Is it that obvious?" I replied sarcastically.

"I thought you writers were capable of chasing a story through any terrain," he snickered.

"We are. We just like to have a little notice first."

They both laughed again. "That is Carter's style," Matt said through his laughter. "He likes to keep people on their toes."

I stomped past them and their laughter into the mess hall, still holding the easel and Jordan's picture. I waited for someone to tell me where to put them, but no one did, so I just leaned them against the wall and took the towel off Jordan's face. His smile beamed out at the room from beside a stack of boxes and chairs. His celebration of life was the reason for this island getaway, but no one seemed to care if his memory was set aside with the rest of the party decorations.

Now that my hands were free, it was time to find a drink. Thankfully, Jackie was digging through a cluster of ice chests in the corner of the room. I walked over to her, hoping the ice chests were filled with beer or something stronger. "Find anything good in there?" I asked.

She jumped at the sound of my voice. "Billy, you scared me," she said, turning around and holding a hand to her chest.

"Oh, yeah, sorry. This is probably not the best party to be sneaking up behind people."

She snorted at my poor joke. "Want a beer?"

"Yes, please. Whose beer is it?"

"It's communal," she answered. "Everyone brings drinks to share with the club. It would be a cold day in hell if this place ever ran out of alcohol."

That sounded like my style of yacht club. Jackie handed me a dark bottle of beer, and we cheersed. "Are you still mad at me?" she asked. "I swear I didn't know we were coming here when I texted you."

"It's OK, Jackie. I'm on an island with the most exclusive yacht club in San Diego and an endless supply of free beer. I've faced worse circumstances."

Jackie smiled. "OK, good. I still feel bad, but I'll try to stop feeling like I trapped you."

The screen door beside us swung open, and a guy with a long beard strolled through. After a moment, I realized it was Joe. He froze when he saw us. He was wearing black capri pants and a black shirt with the name of some band on it. His beard looked just as grizzly as it had on the night of Jordan's murder. "Hello, Jackie," he said with a strained voice.

"Hello, Joe," she replied coldly.

They both glared at each other without saying another word. I looked back and forth between them, wondering who would give in first. I had never seen Jackie like this before. When she told me about Joe getting fired from the office, she made it seem like she didn't care. Now, her back was arched, and her claws were bared.

Jackie spoke first. "I didn't think you'd be here, Joe."

"It's a club event, right?" Joe grumbled. "All hands on deck is what the email said. Otherwise, I'd pay to be anywhere else right now."

Joe's attention shifted to me. "This guy again? New boyfriend?" He chuckled as if it were a joke and grabbed a beer from an ice chest. "This must be hard for you, Jackie. Two memorials in just over a year. That's some real bad luck." He chuckled again and sauntered out the door.

Jackie's usually soft brown cheeks were flushed red; her eyes could have set a propane tank on fire. I couldn't tell if she was lost in memory or fighting back emotions. I opened the beer in my hand and offered it to her, but she didn't seem to notice.

"Joe seems like a lovely guy," I said. "He's been showing up a lot lately."

"He's a member of the yacht club by extension of his father," Jackie said. "Whenever the club has a big meeting or ceremony like this, all members are required to attend, or they could get kicked out of the club."

"Sounds like a harsh consequence for skipping a memorial."

Jackie shrugged. "I guess that's how you stay exclusive."

"What did he mean about two memorials?"

"I don't want to talk about it," Jackie snapped. She hesitated for a second, then stomped out the door without another word. I looked around at the now silent mess hall and realized my wildest nightmare had come true—being alone on an isolated island with an endless supply of free beer and a killer on the loose.

15

J ordan's memorial service was scheduled to start at 3 p.m. Everyone packed into the mess hall to pay their final respects and maintain their facades. Laughter, booze, and the scent of sunscreen mixed with tanning oils filled the room. One gentleman didn't even bother to wear a shirt. His protruding belly had been tanned to leather, and the hair on his chest was gray. He carried around a bowl of chicken wings, offering them to the crowd. To my horror, people actually grabbed the wings and tore the meat off the bones like wild animals in the bush. The whole scene made me feel claustrophobic.

A woman stepped up to the microphone at the front of the room and announced that the service would start in two minutes. The crowd began shuffling to their chairs, but the chatter and laughter continued. Kylie was the only one not looking for a chair. She checked her phone and then went outside. I already knew what the script readers would say about Jordan and his ambition for life, so I quietly excused myself and followed Kylie out of the service.

She was sitting at a table on the porch when I got outside. She couldn't have been older than twenty. She had blonde hair that might have been dyed and tanned skin that could have been artificial. She looked up from her phone when she heard me come out.

"I'm glad I'm not the only one who could use some fresh air," I said.

"Are you here for Jordan's celebration?" she asked, as if there could be any other reason for me to be here.

"Yes. I'm Billy. Do you mind if I sit for a second?"

If my intrusion bothered her, she didn't let on. She pointed to the other side of the table. "Please, sit down. Were you friends with Jordan?"

"Not really," I replied, sitting down to face her. "I met him the night of the party."

"Oh, so you were there when it happened?"

"I was."

The weight of my words lingered between us for a moment. She looked past me toward the ocean, but there were no tears in her eyes. Maybe she had already cried out all of her tears, or maybe she wasn't the crying type.

"I'm sorry," I said, "I didn't catch your name." I felt phony for lying, but phony wasn't as bad as creepy.

"I'm Kylie."

"It's nice to meet you, Kylie. Did you know Jordan well?"

"You could say that. We've actually been dating for about a year." She gave a small smile and a quick shrug as if it were no big deal.

The length of their relationship surprised me. I couldn't imagine enduring Jordan and his antics for an entire year. "I'm sorry for your loss," I said. "It must be hard losing him so suddenly."

She responded to my condolences with another small smile. "I guess it hasn't really hit me yet. I keep thinking it's just one of Jordan's pranks, and he's going to show up out of the blue and laugh at us."

"That would be an evil prank."

"Yes, it would be, but it sounds like Jordan. It would've made him happy to see the look on our faces when he walked through the door."

I explained my actions at the pool and my role as an investigative journalist. She maintained eye contact with me while I spoke, but her phone dinged multiple times, and her hand twitched each time it did. It was like an extension of herself, a sort of robotic appendage she could physically manipulate, but it, in turn, controlled her nervous system.

"When was the last time you saw Jordan?" I asked.

"The day of his party," Kylie answered. "We were at his condo before he got picked up by the party bus. I was supposed to go, but I wasn't feeling well."

"How was he acting when you were with him?"

"Normal. Happy," she said, shrugging her shoulders again. "He was excited about the party."

"I assume he was happy because of his promotion?"

Kylie nodded. "I think so. He kept saying that his time had finally come; that he had been waiting years for this moment. I assumed he was talking about his promotion, but I don't really understand why it made him so happy."

Jordan must have kept his smuggling operation a secret from his girlfriend. Maybe she wouldn't have approved. Or maybe she was a better liar than Jordan and had already perfected the disguise of innocence.

"Was it just the two of you getting ready?" I asked.

"Yes. I went to his condo to get ready, but I couldn't work up the energy to go. So I just hung out there until he got picked up, and then I went home and fell asleep. When I woke up the next morning, I had a bunch of missed calls and texts saying Jordan was dead. I didn't believe it until the cops showed up at my door."

Part of me felt sorry for her. Even if her mannerisms didn't show that she cared, it must have been hard to lose someone so tragically—unless she planned it, of course. The thought of losing Jewels flashed through my mind, but I pushed it aside before it could take hold of my emotions.

"Kylie, I have to ask, why did you leave the celebration to come out here?"

She pursed her lips and cast a sideways glance at me. "Have you met Jordan's dad and the people he works with?"

"I have."

"Then you know this is all just for show, and I already put on enough of a show in my life."

Her blunt insight caught me off guard. Despite being so young and flamboyant, she seemed to possess a keen awareness of her surroundings. Years of online exposure and trying to impress others probably taught her many survival skills, including how to read people and understand their motives.

I decided to skip to the point. "Did Jordan ever say anything about making some extra money?"

"You mean like a side hustle?"

"Something like that."

Kylie scrunched up her face in thought. "I don't think so. He always talked about running the company someday and making it the biggest real estate business on the West Coast. He made it sound like it would happen tomorrow."

"Did you believe him?"

"I don't know," she sighed. "Jordan said a lot of things that were bigger than reality. But he believed it."

"Did he mention how he planned to grow the company?"

Kylie didn't answer right away. She was either thinking about my question or judging my interest in her deceased boyfriend. "It seems to me, Billy, like you already have some ideas of your own," she said finally.

"Not necessarily," I replied, a bit thrown off by her response. "I'm just trying to connect the dots and validate a potential lead in his murder."

"I can't tell you anything more right now," she said, standing up from the table. "I should probably get back to the celebration. I don't want to give everyone another reason to gossip about me."

"Yes. Right. I'm sorry for keeping you. Could we talk again when we're back in San Diego?"

"Sure," she said with a smile. She had a good smile. "It's not that I mind the questions. I just don't think we should do this here. I'm supposed to go out with some of my girls Thursday night; you're welcome to stop by my apartment before then."

I told her that would be great, and she gave me her address. She didn't seem nervous about sharing such personal information with someone she had just met. She checked her makeup with her phone and wiped the sand off her dress. Then I opened the door of the mess hall for her, and she glided in like she was the queen of the island.

———

After the ceremony, everyone scattered from the mess hall like a shaken beehive. Everyone seemed to have something better to do than sit around and offer their condolences. Nancy and Jackie were the only faces I recognized who stayed behind.

I wanted to say something to them, but I couldn't find any words worth saying.

I grabbed a beer from the alcohol stash and went out to the back patio. The hill behind the camp was barren except for a few gnarled bushes, but it blocked most of the wind that hounded the mainland. I was halfway through the beer when Joe walked by, headed toward the cabins. I chugged the rest of my drink and hurried over to him. "Excuse me, Joe?" I called out.

He turned to see who had called his name, then continued walking when he realized it was me. I caught up and fell into step beside him. "Hey, Joe, I'm not the guy you think I am," I said, only slightly out of breath. "I just met these people the other day."

He stopped walking and turned to me with an annoyed look. "You seem pretty friendly with them, though."

I raised my hands to show my innocence. "I was just a victim of happenstance."

"That's an odd way to put it," Joe smirked.

"Look, I already had a room at the Blue Swan on the night of Jordan's party. I was eating dinner at the bar when you guys showed up—"

"Hold up," Joe interrupted. "I didn't go to the motel with them."

"OK, fine. I was there when their party bus showed up. They stormed into the bar like a pack of wild dogs. They bought me a few drinks, we talked for a while, and then I called it a night. Later, I went down to the front desk for some Advil, saw Jordan in the pool, and jumped in without thinking. You know the rest."

"And now you're here," he said, motioning with his hand toward the island. "Why?"

"I work for an investigative magazine. My editor told me to cover the story, or I'd be fired."

He processed my explanation slowly, probably searching for any sign of lies. His past had conditioned him to hate these people and anyone connected to them. I wondered why he spent so much time with people he clearly despised. "What do you want from me?" he asked.

"I understand you used to work at the company?"

"That's common knowledge."

"And you got let go because of a disagreement with Jordan?"

"Not a disagreement. I got fired because Jordan was a liar."

"That doesn't sound very fair to me," I coaxed.

"I'm over it," Joe huffed, but the tone of his voice suggested otherwise.

"Mind if I ask what Jordan lied about?"

His eyes narrowed. "Mind if I ask whether this conversation will be part of your story?"

"I don't know, maybe. But if there's nothing to it, then there's no need for the cops to get involved." I hoped the threat of police involvement would be enough to make him talk.

"Are you working with the cops too?" he asked.

"No."

"Then what would they want from me?"

"I don't know. But I assume they'll come knocking once they find out you were at the scene of the crime and have a history with the victim."

"I have nothing to hide," Joe growled.

"Look, Jordan had a wild streak in him; we all know that. Hell, he was brandishing a sword in public within the first hour I met him. I can only imagine how frustrating it was to work with him every day and then get fired because he lied to his dad—"

Joe cut me off again. "No. You're fishing, and it won't work. I don't know why you're trying to paint this fantastical picture of a motive for me to kill Jordan, but I had absolutely nothing to do with it."

"Then why were you at the party?" I snapped back. "I understand club members are required to be here on the island for the memorial. But Jordan's party wasn't a club requirement."

Joe turned as if he was about to walk away, but then spun back around. He pointed his finger at my chest. The anger he had bottled up in his soul was now spilling out. "Who has been feeding you information? Is it Jackie? It looked like there was something intimate between you guys."

My journalistic instincts told me not to reveal my source, but there was no point in trying to hide the obvious. "Yes," I answered. "Jackie has been filling me in on some details of the company. But any relationship you might perceive between us is strictly professional."

He scoffed at my comment. "Be careful how much you trust Jackie. She has her own skeletons in the closet."

"What does that mean?" I asked skeptically.

"Oh, she hasn't told you?" He let out a short laugh that wasn't real. "So then she hasn't shared all of the company secrets."

Now it was my turn to be humbled by his words. I'd chosen to believe that Jackie was on my side and that she wanted to find the killer among us. But if she had been feeding me biased information, then I'd been playing the fool all along. "I'm listening," I said.

Joe smiled wickedly. "You're in for a treat, Mr. Investigative Journalist. Jackie used to date a guy named Benji, who was a member of the yacht club. Benji would bring Jackie to club outings, and they seemed like a great couple at first. But rumors began to spread that Jackie wasn't entirely faithful in their relationship. Rumor had it that she was seeing someone in the club. Tempers flared. People argued and blamed each other. Benji said he was done with the club. Then, one day, he simply disappeared off the face of the map. A week later, Jackie got a job working at the Carter Real Estate Company."

I did my best to keep a straight face during Joe's soliloquy. I didn't want to give him the satisfaction of seeing any reaction from me. "What happened to Benji?" I asked when he was done.

"No one knows," Joe replied with a satisfied grin. "One day, he was here, and the next day, he and his boat were gone. The cops investigated his disappearance but never found anything. He is still considered a missing person to this day."

"What did Jackie say about his disappearance?"

Joe snorted. "She played the part. She cried and told everyone how much she loved him. But once she started working at the office, I never heard her mention his name again. If you ask me, I'd say she wasn't sad at all that Benji was gone."

I scratched my head and looked around the resort. An older couple emerged from a cabin, sipping from colorful cups and laughing like they were teenagers again. They raised their cups in the air and waved them at another couple walking by. Everyone seemed happy, rich, and drunk.

Joe must have recognized my thoughts because he shook his head. "I'm telling you, these people can't be trusted."

"Were there any names linked to the rumors about who else Jackie was seeing?" I asked.

Joe's satisfied grin returned. "No one ever admitted to it. But everyone had the same suspicion."

"Which was?" I hated playing his game of cat and mouse, but he had taken control of the conversation and was happy to string me along.

"Carter," he whispered, then looked around to make sure no one was within earshot. "He took a liking to her right away. They would even flirt right in front of Benji. Benji eventually confronted Carter about it at a club party and made a big scene. That was the last night we all saw Benji. And like I said, just a week later, Jackie was sitting at the front desk of the Carter Real Estate Company." He paused for a moment to let his story sink in. "You do the math, Billy."

I did the math. It didn't add up well. "What does any of this have to do with you being at the Blue Swan on the night Jordan was murdered?"

"I'm just trying to warn you about who you are getting involved with," he answered. But I knew it wasn't altruism that powered his warnings.

"You're deflecting, Joe. And you'll be part of this story until you come clean yourself."

Joe's face sagged a little when he realized his warnings hadn't sent me running to the closest boat back to the mainland. "Where there is money, there are powerful people," he said, glancing around again to make sure none of those powerful people were standing behind him. "And powerful people don't like to lose their money."

I followed his wandering eyes as he scanned the cabins. "Do you think we're being watched?"

"I don't know, but something's not right," he answered. "These people, they would do anything to make an extra buck or to keep what they have. They saw me as a threat, so they kicked me out."

"Then help me out, Joe. I'm here to find out what happened to Jordan."

Joe shrugged and sighed. He started walking again, but this time more slowly, and I followed beside him. "OK," he said after a dramatic pause. "I was there to find out what Jordan was doing with his listings."

An alarm went off in my head. "What do you mean?"

"He was doing weird things with his listings," Joe answered. "He would put a house on the market, then take it off, and then put it back up a couple of days later. He would price houses way too high. Things just seemed odd to me."

"Odd, like he didn't know what he was doing? Or odd, like he was doing something suspicious?"

"Suspicious," Joe replied. "I might not have liked the guy, but he knew how to sell houses. So his behavior was curious, to say the least."

"Sounds like you were keeping tabs on him."

Joe bobbed his head from side to side, as if weighing his actions and motivations. "I guess you could say that. I know it looks bad to admit it, but I held a grudge against Jordan. He took a lot of money from me, and I wanted to do the same to him. I wanted to find out what he was doing and report it so that he'd lose his license."

"So you showed up to the party to confront him about his listing protocols?" I asked. "It wouldn't have made a great environment to conduct an interrogation."

"Yes, I know," Joe said. "But Jordan was bound to get hammered and boisterous at his own party. I thought maybe he'd slip up and say something he shouldn't, or maybe the other guys in the office would mention something. I'm not allowed at the office anymore, so the party was my best chance to find out what was going on."

"Did you get a chance to confront him?"

"Yes, but he got angry and denied doing anything strange, which made me even more suspicious."

"Suspicious of what, though?" I asked. "Why would he be listing houses like you say he was?"

"I don't know," Joe answered. "That's what I wanted to find out. But that doesn't make me a killer."

We reached his cabin. He stopped at the bottom of the stairs and put one hand on the railing to block me. "You're really just a writer?" he asked.

"Yes."

"And you didn't bring anything to the island to protect yourself?"

"Should I have?"

"Well, someone murdered Jordan, and chances are the murderer is on this island, and the only protection you have is the clothes on your back."

My spine itched, and Joe smirked. "I hope to see you alive in the morning, Billy," he said. And with that, he walked up the stairs and into the cabin, closing the door behind him.

16

No one had offered me access to their cabin, so there was nowhere to hide or escape the elements. But I didn't mind for now. The idea of taking a nap on the warm sand under a swaying palm tree sounded wonderful. Toss in a bottle of whiskey and maybe a few darts to throw at people's feet when I was drunk, and I'd be a happy man.

I went back to the mess hall to salvage whatever alcohol was hidden in the treasure chests. Two women were flapping a tablecloth across a table. They smiled at me and said the food would be ready soon. I thanked them and waited until they looked away, then filled my pockets with beers.

I walked out to the porch and flopped into a rocking chair to enjoy my bounty and watch the ocean. Thirty yards down the beach, Kylie was sitting on a boulder surrounded by ankle-high whitewash. Her head was tilted toward the sky, and her back was arched. Her slim white bikini left little to the imagination. Charlie was standing on the sand with a phone pointed at her. After a second, he lowered the phone and just stared. Kylie must have noticed because she broke her pose and said something to him. Charlie quickly raised the phone again, and Kylie puffed out her chest and looked at the ocean over her shoulder.

Just a few yards away from them, two little girls wearing life jackets jumped around in the surf. One of them splashed the other and sent her fleeing away in childish delight. I told myself that if I ever had a daughter, I'd never let her grow up only valuing herself in front of a camera. But then again, I didn't have a great track record of taking care of myself, let alone raising another human being. How would I teach her to be a good person? How would I apologize for all the stupid things I did and put her through?

I chugged the rest of my beer to drown the image of being a father.

I remembered a conversation I'd had at the border with a woman from Nicaragua. Her husband had been robbed and stabbed while walking home from work one night. He died the next day. So she packed a bag for herself and her teenage son, and they headed north. They were passing through Mexico when their bus was hijacked by one of the cartels. The men on the bus were given the choice to join the cartel, but first, they had to prove themselves by fighting each other to the death. The woman's son refused to fight, so they shot him. She said her son had always been good at math and hoped to go to school to become an engineer.

I cracked another beer and finished it in two gulps.

"Hey, Mr. Writer Man," someone called out, interrupting my dark meditations.

I turned around to see Matt and Leah walking toward the mess hall. They had beers in their hands and smiles on their faces. They looked like the happiest people at the happiest place on earth.

"Want to join us for a game of cards?" Matt asked.

My gut reaction said no, but my journalistic instinct and Steve's voice in my head said yes. "What type of cards?"

"Poker. Some of the old men like to play. They're probably drunk enough by now to play loose with their cash."

"What's the buy-in?"

"A couple hundred bucks. No big deal."

"I don't have any cash on me."

"Come with us. One of the old-timers might spot you."

I hesitated. These didn't seem like the type of people I wanted to owe money to.

Leah noticed my hesitation. "It's not the guys you should worry about," she said. "I usually take all their money."

I didn't doubt it. A little smile and a lot of skin would probably make the old men push all their chips in. "OK," I said. "I'll see how long I can last, and I'll pay them back when we get to the mainland."

They chuckled and told me to follow them. We headed to one of the far cabins where Dustin, the fat man who handed out chicken wings, and another old guy I didn't recognize were sitting around a table.

"What the hell is he doing here?" Dustin growled as we walked through the door.

"Oh, don't worry about Billy here," Leah said. "He just wants to donate to my poker fund."

"I would, except I don't have any cash on me," I said.

Dustin snorted. "Can't play without cash."

"I'll cover you, young man," the fat man said with a jolly smile. He was still shirtless, and I imagined his hands were permanently covered in chicken wing sauce. "But if you somehow win, then you owe me half."

"Deal." I pulled out a chair and sat down. It probably should have bothered me more that I was sitting down to play poker with a possible murderer, but to hell with it. It would sound good in my story if I made it out alive.

Dustin did not look happy. Matt sat down next to him and slapped him on the back. "Cheer up, man. This guy is harmless." He looked at me and grinned. I wanted to tell him they should be worried, that I knew more than they thought, but I kept my mouth shut and returned his smile.

We played for an hour. Dustin smacked the table and cursed a few times, the front of Leah's dress dipped lower and lower, and Matt grinned and touched Leah's bare thigh whenever she won a hand. The game moved fast, and Leah's stack of chips grew faster.

At one point during the game, Dustin's phone rang. He checked the screen and immediately folded his hand. "It's about time," he huffed. "I was worried there wouldn't be any service in this shithole of a resort." He hopped up from the table and marched outside before answering the call. Matt's yellow-tinted eyes watched him go.

Before we even finished the hand, Dustin came back in, smiling from ear to ear. "We are all set for the Topanga house," he said, practically jumping back to his seat at the table.

"When?" Matt asked.

"Thursday."

Matt's face cracked into a wide grin. "Hell yeah! Let's go." He clasped hands with Dustin in private celebration.

"Boys!" Leah said, interrupting their revelry.

Both men looked at Leah, then at me. Dustin's face tightened into a glare when he remembered I was still sitting at the table and using up his oxygen. Matt just grinned and laid down his hand. "Let's keep playing, shall we?" he said. "I'm going to take all of Leah's money this time."

First to leave the game was the man I didn't know. He wasn't upset about losing; he was just happy to have been invited. Next was the fat man. He laughed and said something about finding some ribs. I think he forgot he had loaned me two hundred dollars.

That left me with the agents. Dustin was next to go. I called his bluff and put him out on a pair of queens. He smacked the table with both hands and pointed at me. "This fucking guy." His lip twitched, and I thought he was going to say more, but he stood up and stomped out.

Matt laughed when the door slammed behind Dustin. "Poor guy has a temper."

"Is he always like that?" I asked.

Matt continued grinning and watching me through his yellow-tinted glasses. He looked like a cult leader from a video game, and I realized I had called him almost every terrible name a person could be called—devil, feline, and now cult leader—but they all suited him.

"Let's just say Dustin has his moments," Matt said.

I thought about Dustin and Jordan working in the same office and how many times Dustin must have blown a fuse because of Jordan's antics. It was a minor miracle Dustin hadn't already been jailed for murder. "What about you?" I asked. "How long have you been with the company?"

Matt grinned but didn't respond immediately. He wouldn't fall into an interrogation trap as easily as the other agents. "Not long," he finally said. "I've moved around. I like to go where the money goes."

"It sounds like the Carter Real Estate Company makes a lot of money."

"Indeed, we do."

Leah cut in. "Enough jabber, boys. Deal the cards."

We played a few more rounds until I went all in. Leah folded. Matt called my bet and grinned. I flipped over three aces. He flipped over a straight.

"Tough luck, man," he said as he pulled my chips into his pile.

I cursed to myself and sighed. "I'll have to find that guy and pay him."

"He's probably passed out on the beach by now. He won't be hard to find; just look for a big chunk of burned flesh."

I stood up to leave.

"Oh, and Billy," Matt said. "If you keep following us, you're likely to end up just like Jordan."

17

By the time the sun was setting, I had a good head start on a righteous drunk. I was refueling in the mess hall when Leah and Jaselle stumbled through the door. Leah had her arm around Jaselle's back, with her hip pushed out to support Jaselle's weight. Jaselle's eyelids drooped to her cheeks; her mouth opened and closed in inaudible words. Her head slipped off Leah's shoulder, jerked back upright, and then started another downward slide.

"A little help here, please," Leah said through clenched teeth.

I hurried over and reached out to steady Jaselle, but Leah interpreted my gesture as an offer to take the intoxicated woman. She let go of Jaselle before I had a firm hold, and I struggled to catch the incapacitated woman before she fell to the floor.

"Damn woman can't handle her alcohol," Leah said, wiping her hands like she was wiping off Jaselle's germs.

"How'd she get so drunk?" I hoisted Jaselle higher in my arms to get a better grip. She was not a big woman, but her deadweight and muscle spasms made her hard to hold.

Leah gave Jaselle a disgusted look. "I don't know. She and Carter came to our cabin for a drink. Carter left her with us and said he'd be back. But he didn't come back, and I'm not about to babysit a grown woman. So I carried her ass back here to look for Carter. I don't know which cabin is theirs."

"I think I know which cabin is theirs."

"Good, because she isn't my mess to take care of anymore."

"So she's mine?"

Leah's disgusted look flashed to me. "You might as well make yourself useful. Just take her to her cabin and let her sleep it off." She looked back at Jaselle and snorted before marching out of the mess hall, leaving me alone with the drunk woman in my arms.

"Well, shit," I said out loud to no one. Jaselle's head nodded as if she could hear my voice, but there was no form of comprehension capable of penetrating the liquid barrier surrounding her brain. "Try to pick up your feet, Jaselle," I said just to hear the sound of my voice. "Let's try to get you home."

We trudged through the sand with Jaselle's feet leaving skid marks behind us. A few shadows darted between the cabins, but no one stopped to check on Jaselle's health or offer assistance. It was disturbing to think that I could have been dragging Jaselle anywhere, maybe already having driven a sword through her stomach, and no one would have cared or questioned my intentions.

Thankfully, the cabin Jaselle shared with Ross was one of the first ones away from the mess hall. The door opened smoothly when I turned the handle, nearly sending us crashing to the floor.

"Easy there, lady," I said to myself. "We can't just leave you on the floor."

The cabin was dark, with the only light coming from the moon streaming through the windows. On one side of the room, there was a couch and a table; on the other, a small kitchen area. A hallway on the far side extended back into the cabin. I dragged Jaselle's limp body toward the hallway, assuming that's where the bedroom was. We were halfway down the hall when a jolt of electricity shot through Jaselle's nerves. Her sudden movement caught me off guard, and she slipped from my grasp, hitting the wall with a thud. Somehow, she managed to turn on the hallway light before sliding down to the floor.

"You're not going to make this easy, are you?" I said as I reached down to lift her again. Her head rocked from side to side, but her consciousness was far away from the cabin and Catalina Island.

I finally got a firm grip on her arms and lifted her off the floor. The thought crossed my mind that this was the second time in just a few days I had picked someone up like this. It was a troubling pattern that needed to end. I dragged her body into the bedroom. The light from the hallway illuminated the room enough to locate the bed in the corner. I reached out to pull the bedspread off, but something moved under the blankets. My hand jerked back. There was a small lump in the middle of the bed. I reached out again, slower this time, grabbed the top edge of the bedspread, and slowly peeled it back. A coiled snake suddenly lunged at me as the blanket was pulled across its body.

I fell backward, dropping Jaselle like a lifeless mannequin. I kicked myself across the floor and blindly slapped the wall until my hand hit a light switch. Light flooded the room, revealing the snake curled up in the middle of the bed. It was rattling now; its eyes held a biblical hatred. Fortunately, it wasn't a big snake, or its fangs would have sunk into my arm.

I hurried over to Jaselle and pulled her away from the bed, keeping my eyes on the snake the entire time. Its eyes followed me, its tongue flicked at the air, but it didn't move. I lifted Jaselle off the floor and backed out of the room. By the time we reached the porch and descended the stairs, Carter was approaching us from the beach.

"What the hell is going on?" he demanded when he saw Jaselle in my arms.

"There's a snake... in your bed," I panted.

"What the hell are you talking about? What's wrong with my wife?" He had a bottle of liquor in his hands. He set it down at the bottom of the stairs and pulled Jaselle out of my arms.

"I don't know what happened to her," I stammered. "Leah brought her to the mess hall and practically threw her into my arms. I carried her here and almost made it to the bed, but there was a frickin' snake under the covers. It damn near got us, too. If Jaselle hadn't accidentally turned on the hallway light, I probably would have laid her right on top of it."

Carter's face was partly hidden in shadows, but he bristled when I told him his wife had been inches from danger and possible death. "What did the snake look like?"

"It wasn't too big. Light brown with geometric shapes. It didn't rattle until I pulled the blanket off it—"

"Rattlesnakes on this island are very defensive," Carter interrupted. "You must have spooked it."

"Jesus," I said, feeling my heart rate pick up again. "How could it have gotten in?"

Carter shook his head. "I was in here just an hour ago organizing our bedroom. I didn't see it. There's no way it could have gotten into the cabin and into the bed."

His reasoning left only one possible explanation. "Does that mean someone put it there?"

We both scanned the cabins as if another snake might be lurking around any corner. A shiver ran down my spine, and I

checked my arms again just to make sure there were no punc-
ture wounds.

"Take this bottle," Carter said, pointing at the bottle on the
bottom step. "I need to take Jaselle somewhere she'll be safe."

He strode away, carrying Jaselle's lifeless body in his arms. I
glanced back at the still-open cabin door, grabbed the bottle of
whiskey from the stairs, and hurried away to find a quiet place
to drink.

———

That evening, the true beasts of the island emerged. Grown
men, movers and shakers of society, danced around the flames
like cavemen, their primitive nature exposed by the island, the
sea, and the liquor. Their bonfires crackled and pushed to the
edge of their pits, fighting with the devil's strength to break
free from their concrete entrapments. The shadows of the
dancers were elongated and demonic on the sand. They spun
in circles and howled at the moon.

The bottle of whiskey Carter had given me was half empty
and stuck in the sand at my feet. I picked it up by the neck
and chugged. Jackie appeared out of the darkness and sat down
on the log beside me. The outline of her body flickered in the
shadows of the fire and the stupor in my brain.

She laughed at the sight of me. "What a night, huh, Billy?"

"Sure," I blurted out. "We're on a beautiful island with a
bunch of lunatic yachtsmen, miles away from anywhere or
anything sane."

She laughed again. "Are you always so dreary?"

"I think it runs in my profession. And I'm a professional if
nothing else."

"Yes, you are," she chuckled and bumped shoulders with me.

We sat in silence for a minute, watching the gluttons on the beach. Some of the wives and girlfriends had joined the fray. I took another drink from the bottle and said something about being rich. Jackie said I was too nice to be rich and took the bottle from my hands. She took a sip and was seized by a fit of coughing. I grabbed the bottle back before she dropped it and poured out good whiskey onto the sand.

"What's life like at home, Billy?" she asked after she stopped coughing.

"It's good," I replied. I couldn't think of anything else to say.

"That's it? Just good? Do you have anyone waiting for you at home?"

"Yes, I do. But I don't deserve to. I'm not sure why she sticks with me."

"What's her name?"

"Julianna. She goes by Jewels."

"That's cute," Jackie said, but I couldn't tell if she meant it. "How long have you two been together?"

"A couple of years, I think. There are stretches of days or weeks when I'm not home much, so it's hard to keep track of time."

Jackie snorted at my response. "Yeah, I can see why she'd get mad at you. How did you two meet?"

"She was a teacher at a school I was writing about. It was a reform school for children with emotional disorders. She taught sixth grade. On the day I visited the school, she had to restrain a student in her class who was trying to throw a desk at another student. She had to help that same student with his math work later in the day."

"Wow," Jackie said. "She sounds amazing."

"She is amazing, and that's why I don't understand how she stays with me."

We fell silent again. Jewels's presence hung between us from hundreds of miles away. I took another sip from the whiskey bottle and waited for the taste to fade. Then I spoke carefully. "Jackie, I need to ask you something."

"What's that?"

"It's about Benji."

I sensed her body stiffen. She looked at me, and the firelight and shadows danced across her face. "Please tell me you haven't been talking to people about Benji," she said. "You know how rumors can replace the truth when people talk too much."

"That's true. But it's my job to pursue both rumors and truth."

Jackie's face twisted like she wanted to spit at me. "Fine," she said sharply. "Ask your questions."

I hesitated. We had reached a crossroads that would shape our future interactions and might ultimately affect my ability to cover this story. Jackie had played a crucial role in helping me get to this point. If I lost her trust now, I'd probably lose her support going forward.

"What happened to him?" I asked.

"I don't know," Jackie chirped.

"You must have some suspicion, though."

Jackie didn't answer right away. She turned away from me and stared at the fires and into the past. The flames reflecting on her face made it impossible to read her emotions. She sighed, picked up the bottle, and took a heavy slug. This time, she didn't cough.

"Benji told me he was taking the boat out," she said slowly. "We had been fighting. I figured he just needed some time to cool down, and he'd be gone for an afternoon or maybe a day.

But a day passed, and then another, and then he never came back."

"Was his boat ever located?"

"Yes. But he wasn't." She picked up the bottle again and raised it to her lips, but then set it back down without taking a drink.

"What were you fighting about?" I asked when she didn't say anything else.

"Why do you ask questions you already know the answers to?" she snapped. "It's really fucking annoying."

Her anger made my breath catch. It was new to me, and I wasn't sure how to navigate it. "I'm sorry, Jackie. I just want to hear your side of the story."

"Did they tell you I was sleeping with someone else?" she snapped, flicking her hands angrily as she spoke. "Maybe even that I was involved with Benji's disappearance?"

When I didn't answer, she continued. "I know what everyone says about me—that I was hooking up with someone in the club, that Benji caught on, and then he disappeared. Is that what you think happened, Billy?" She leaned forward, daring me to answer.

I wanted to believe her, and part of me did, but the drunk part of me responded to her question. "I obviously don't know what happened."

It was the wrong thing to say. Jackie stood up and thrust the whiskey bottle at me. "Here you go, Billy. Keep drinking till you find your answers." She dropped the bottle in my lap. "I thought you were a good guy, but now I realize you're just like everyone else. Maybe even worse, because you think you can just sit back and judge everyone else's lives."

"Jackie, I'm sorry. I was just—"

"Stop, Billy. Just stop," she interrupted, pumping both hands at me like she was building a wall between us. "I tried to be nice. I tried to help you figure out what happened to Jordan. And now you want to grill me about a man I loved who has been missing for over a year? Really? I'm not going to do it."

"Jackie, I'm sorry," I repeated. "I was just trying to piece it together in my mind."

"There's nothing to piece together. Benji is gone. We don't know what happened to him, and it breaks my heart every day to think about it. He should be here right now." Then she pointed at me. "You shouldn't be, though. You don't belong here. I should have never invited you to Jordan's party and into our lives."

"Jackie," I mumbled.

"No!" she snapped. "Don't talk to me. Have a nice fucking night."

She stormed off and vanished into the shadows of the island. I wondered if my questions had offended her because they were based on rumors or truth. Either way, a wall had formed between us. I took another pull from the bottle. Even in a yacht club where people danced around their fires with wild abandon, I found a way to be alone with the night and my whiskey.

18

I woke up the next morning with my face in the sand and an empty whiskey bottle beside me. The sun was already well above the horizon of the mainland. I pushed myself up and tried to brush the sand off my face and out of my hair. My mouth tasted like I'd gargled a pitcher of ocean water and whiskey. My body felt like someone had rolled me down the side of a mountain.

People were scurrying around the beach and loading bags into dinghies. Some were already making the trip from the shore to their boats. A guy I didn't recognize shuffled past me with an ice chest. He didn't stop or look down as he passed within a foot of my outstretched legs.

I caught sight of Carter loading his dinghy at the shoreline. Dustin, Matt, and Leah were just stepping into the raft. I stood up on wobbly legs and hurried over as quickly as I could, waving my hands over my head to get their attention, but it felt like I was moving in slow motion through the sand. The entire scene could have unfolded like a dramatic escape in a World War II film. Hopefully, I was the injured soldier who made it out in time, not the one who got blown up on the verge of rescue.

Carter was pushing the dinghy off the sand when I finally caught up to them. I waded into the surf and jumped onto the raft just as the water began to pick up its weight. The three agents looked at me, but none of them said a word. I figured they would have been just fine leaving me stranded on the island.

We reached the Lynn Dixie, and I tried to lift an ice chest up to the yacht, but my hands were trembling, and the handle slipped from my grasp. Carter grabbed the ice chest and loaded it onto the boat without saying anything. I climbed aboard, found a seat in the cabin, and pulled my jacket tightly around me. The morning wasn't really cold, but I felt vulnerable and fragile.

We rode back to the mainland in silence. The reverie and exposure from the night before weighed down our emotions and imprisoned us each in our own memories and justifications. The only person who spoke to me was Nancy, who had skipped the bonfires to retire early to her cabin. She asked if I had learned anything new. I told her that I had, but that the knowledge had actually muddied my investigation of her son's murder. Nancy looked saddened by my admission, like maybe she had put too much hope in me.

Once, I thought I was going to be sick and ran out to the deck to lean over the edge, but I held it in. I stayed on the deck and let the sun and wind soothe my nerves. It also helped to watch the contours of the mainland in the distance and imagine being on solid ground. My mind drifted to Jewels. She was probably at work right now, helping a student with their spelling or talking to another teacher about her no-good boyfriend. She'd probably stop at the store on her way home to get a bottle of wine and some grocery store sushi. She'd check her phone before she went to sleep tonight and wonder where I was. She deserved better than me.

But out here, in the middle of the waves, nothing seemed to matter. Maybe that's why people chose a life on the water. You could observe the faults of humanity and pass judgment from afar. You could keep your distance from the tragedies and wretchedness of living next to your fellow man. And if trouble ever did arise on the high seas, you could just throw it overboard and keep sailing toward a new horizon.

19

When we arrived at the Statesman Yacht Club, everyone quickly gathered their belongings and raced off the boat. I tried to help Jackie with her bag, but she said she could carry it herself. So I waited for the rest of the group to leave, then took off Carter's jacket, set it on a table, and vowed never to join a yacht club.

An employee in a baby blue polo and white slacks asked if he could help carry my bags to the clubhouse. He looked confused when I told him I didn't have any, but he quickly regained his composure and said cheerfully, "Have a happy day, sir." I hurried up the dock, through the clubhouse, down the driveway, and past the security kiosk, where the same old security guard was stationed. It felt like a hundred eyes were watching me the whole way. It felt like the ultimate walk of shame.

I walked the couple of blocks to the corner parking lot to retrieve my car, praying it hadn't been towed or spray-painted by a deranged maniac in the middle of the night. The sun was hot and reflected off everything too brightly. The sounds of the city and the hum of traffic created a cacophony of urban chaos. Twenty-four hours ago, I had felt like anything was possible, like the fresh air and eternal sunshine could heal all wounds and inspire every dream. Now, that excitement was buried deep in the sand on a remote island off the California coast.

When I reached the parking lot, I removed the parking ticket from the window and drove back to the Blue Swan. It was just before noon when I pulled in, and all I wanted was a pillow and maybe a drink to ease my hangover and wobbly knees. But a man and woman, both wearing jackets and ties, stopped me before I made it up the stairs.

"Billy Burnes?" the woman asked. I remembered her from the morning of Jordan's death. She was the detective who had come to my door to speak to Officer Bennett.

"Yes?"

"I'm Detective Pratt," she said, holding up a badge. "This is Detective Mayfield. We'd like to ask you a few questions."

Detective Pratt had bright red hair and serious eyes. She exuded the composure of an experienced detective who had seen the worst of people. Detective Mayfield was past his prime, with gray hair and a sagging body.

"What's this regarding?" I asked, trying to sound naive. I had crossed paths with detectives before and tended to ruffle their feathers. One had even threatened to ruin me. I wasn't sure if he had meant professionally, physically, or both.

"The death of Jordan Carter," Pratt said. She clearly wasn't in the mood for small talk.

"Hey, I already spoke to Officer Bennett. He seems like a swell guy. Why don't you ask him?"

"We want to hear it from you," Pratt replied.

I looked back and forth between the two detectives, but Pratt's face was unreadable, and Mayfield's was too droopy to show normal human emotions. "OK," I sighed. "But can we please make it quick? I really need some sleep."

"Long night?" Pratt asked.

Let's see, I thought to myself, being lured and trapped at a remote island resort, playing poker with potential murderers, barely escaping the fangs of a venomous snake, and waking up with a gut full of sand and liquor. I think that qualified for a long night. "Something like that," was all I responded. "Where would you like to talk?"

"Somewhere quiet will do."

I didn't want to impose on the Swan's hospitality by conducting an interview in the restaurant, so I told them we could talk in my room. They followed me upstairs and silently waited while I fished out the room key and opened the door. They stepped into the room behind me and closed the door.

I hurried to gather the empty beer bottles and whiskey shooters scattered across the room. The detectives looked around with probing eyes as I scurried back and forth to the small trash can under the desk, but it was already full of empties, and the bottles kept rolling off. So I stacked them on the floor next to the trash like some kind of alcoholic shrine and prayed the detectives wouldn't pass too harsh a judgment.

"Sorry," I said. "Lonely nights—you know what I mean?"

"Sure," Detective Pratt replied. Maybe she understood lonely nights, or maybe she knew the habits of lonely men.

When I finished tidying up the room, I sat down on the edge of the bed. Detective Pratt pulled the desk chair over and sat facing me. Detective Mayfield stood by the door, his beady little eyes staring at me through rolls of skin.

"So, Mr. Burnes," Pratt said, pulling out a small notebook from the inside pocket of her jacket. "We've been told you're writing a column about Jordan's death."

"Not really," I shrugged. "I haven't written much."

"Care to tell us what you have written?"

"Just a summary of the night Jordan was killed," I replied. I didn't feel like going into a full explanation of my investigation. My patience and brain power were too thin to recount details I had already reported to the police.

"OK. Is there anything we should know about in your summary?"

"Probably not. I've already told Officer Bennett my account of what transpired."

Pratt took a deep breath and nodded slowly. Her patience was also wearing thin, but she handled it better than I did. "I imagine there was some heavy drinking involved in your summary," she said after glancing around the room again.

"Heavy depends on a person's tolerance," I responded sarcastically.

Detective Mayfield took offense to my tone. "We don't need your snark responses," he snapped. "Just answer the questions." He shifted his excessive weight from one foot to the other but didn't step away from the door. I don't know whether he thought I would try to flee or if he was afraid to get himself dirty by stepping further into the room.

"Let me rephrase the question," Detective Pratt said calmly. "Did Jordan appear intoxicated on the night of his murder?"

I thought about Jordan pounding tequila shots. "Sure, he might have been a little drunk."

"And did he seem intoxicated when he had the sword?" Pratt asked.

"Yes, but not incoherent."

"So you're saying he was incoherent later in the night?"

"I can't say for certain if he was ever incoherent. The whole group was pounding shots, and Jordan was matching anyone who ordered a drink. But I don't remember him stumbling, or mumbling, or anything like that. He was more so loud and obnoxious."

Pratt jotted something down in her notebook. "Do you think drugs were involved?"

"That's possible," I said, even though I already suspected it was true. "It could explain his hyped-up energy after knocking back so many shots."

Pratt took a second to scribble another note. I fought the urge to laugh and tell her she looked like an amateur detective from a 1950s film.

"OK," she said when she finished writing. "Tell us more about your role in this whole thing. How did you get lucky enough to get involved?"

I shrugged again to downplay any role I had at the party. "Luck has never been one of my defining qualities. I was just staying here for the night, and their party showed up and interrupted my dinner."

"But you decided to party with them?" She looked around the room again and at the stack of empty beer bottles in the corner. "I bet they didn't have to twist your arm."

"Listen, I had no intention of joining their party, but they eventually roped me in. We had a few drinks, and then I called it a night. I woke up around 4 a.m. and found the desk clerk standing over Jordan's body."

"And now you're investigating the murder yourself?" Her voice was calm, but she was definitely on the prowl for holes in my story.

"Well, unfortunately, my editor threatened my livelihood if I didn't look into it."

"So your editor instructed you to interfere with a criminal investigation?"

"No. Not at all," I said, trying to avoid digging myself into a hole. "He instructed me to write about the event like any journalist would."

"So, my question is again: have you found anything worth sharing with us?"

I hesitated to respond. Detective Mayfield, the prickly lard that he was, didn't like my pause. "We could book you right now for interfering with an active investigation," he barked. "You need to tell us everything you know."

I resisted the urge to laugh again. "Now I understand why it's taking the cops so long to solve this case," I said. "Cops like you are all guts and no brains."

Mayfield's cheeks somehow bulged even more. He took a step toward me. "Well, aren't you a little fucking prick," he hissed.

"Alright. Easy," Pratt said, as she held her arm up in front of Mayfield. "Just answer the questions, please, Mr. Burnes. We are trying to solve this case as quickly as possible. If you have anything useful, we would greatly appreciate it."

Detective Mayfield continued to stare me down, but he took a step back toward the door. The encounter revealed a lot about Detective Pratt. Guys like Mayfield liked to be in charge, and they wanted everyone to know they were in charge. His quick deference to Pratt showed his respect for her. Maybe she was actually a cop I could work with, and maybe being a team player would actually benefit me for once.

"Alright," I said. "I think Jordan was involved in some sort of drug smuggling scheme. But I don't have much evidence besides testimony from an informant."

"Care to tell us who this informant is?" Pratt asked.

"I told them I would leave their name out."

Pratt scribbled in her notebook. "That information could really help us, Mr. Burnes."

"I don't know what to tell you," I said, shaking my head. "I'm a man of my word."

Pratt took a deep breath through her nose. "Fine. Did they tell you where this smuggling scheme was operating?"

"They did."

Pratt waited for me to say more, but I let my answer dangle between us. After a few seconds, she took another deep breath and asked if I could elaborate.

"I will, if you tell me one thing."

"Which is?" she asked, raising her eyebrows at my audacity to question the police.

I wasn't feeling too confident myself, especially without a belly full of whiskey, and I tried not to let it show on my face. "Were there any fingerprints on the sword handle?"

"Why do you think I would answer that?" Pratt asked in response.

"Because you probably want the information I have, and I'd like to know if you already have a smoking gun."

Pratt paused for a moment to consider my proposal. "No, we weren't able to lift any identifiable prints."

"Does that mean someone wiped it clean?"

"Maybe. But it's more likely that the thin cord wrapped around the handle couldn't hold any prints." She paused after finishing her explanation. "Now, where was this drug operation taking place?"

"One more question. What about the cameras? The night clerk said they only face the pool and the entrance. Did they catch anything?"

Pratt looked at me without expression. I held her gaze. "You're a pain to work with, aren't you?" she said. It wasn't a question.

"I've been called worse."

"Fine. The entrance camera caught Jordan leaving the motel but never returning. The pool camera recorded him falling into the pool. Now, tell me where the drug operation was taking place."

"In the empty houses Jordan was selling."

Detective Pratt took a moment to process the information. Her lips puckered into a thoughtful expression as she scribbled in her notepad. "Tell me more," she said once she finished her private assessment.

I told her the story Dereon shared with me about Jordan using the property listings as stash houses and no longer being satisfied as the middleman. He had been searching for opportunities to distribute the drugs himself, which probably upset the chain of command.

Detective Pratt listened intently while I spoke. "This could be valuable information," she said. "If Jordan was trying to cut people out of the deal, that would make a compelling motive for murder."

"Agreed," I said, nodding to show I could be a good teammate.

"Do you know if anyone else was involved?"

My journalist instincts warned me again not to reveal all of my information, but being a good teammate meant speaking up when I didn't want to. "I can't say for certain, but some of the other agents at the Carter Real Estate Company might have their hands in the cookie jar."

Pratt took a deep breath and held it. I imagined she did a lot of yoga with all the heavy breathing she was doing. I glanced at Detective Mayfield, but he still looked angry or confused.

Pratt let her breath out, leaned forward, and put her hands on her knees. "Please wait one minute, Mr. Burnes, while my partner and I discuss something outside." She motioned to Mayfield, and the two detectives stepped into the hallway. They left the door slightly ajar, and I could hear them arguing. After a minute, only Detective Pratt was doing the talking. They came back in and resumed their positions.

"Listen, Mr. Burnes," Pratt said. "We want to thank you for the information you've provided us. But if this really is a drug smuggling scheme, then it could be a very dangerous situation. I need you to be very careful, and I need you to report anything more you find directly to me."

"Yes, ma'am," I said, but I wasn't sure if I'd follow through with her orders. Pratt sounded genuinely concerned and seemed to be one of the few competent detectives I'd met, but she also hadn't ordered me to end my investigation. That meant she wanted to use me, and detectives didn't care about casting people aside if it meant closing a case.

"And remember," Pratt continued, "this is an active criminal investigation, and interfering with our investigation or withholding information can be used against you in court."

I wanted to say something sarcastic back, but I thought better of it. The parameters of our relationship had been established: report directly to her, or face legal consequences. I'd been in worse relationships.

"One more thing," I said.

"What's that?" she asked, giving me the "don't push your luck, buddy" look.

"Does the name Benji Steadman sound familiar?"

Pratt thought about it for a second. "Yes, it does. What have you heard?"

"Just rumors. I know he was dating someone who is currently working for the Carter Real Estate Company, and that he went missing about a year ago. Did the police ever find anything more?"

Pratt looked at Mayfield, but he just shrugged and shook his head. I wondered if he was an actual detective or if he had won some contest at a charity event to play detective for a day.

"I was working in LA at the time," Pratt answered. "But if I remember correctly, his boat capsized off the coast of Baja. His body was never recovered. As of now, the case is still open." She paused. "Do you have any new information?"

"No. I'm just trying to find out if there's a connection between Benji's disappearance and Jordan's murder."

Pratt glanced at her watch and stood up. She pulled out a business card, flipped it over, and scribbled on the back. "This is my office number and my personal number," she said, handing me the card. "Call me if you find anything else."

I told her again that I would.

Then she tore the top paper out of her notebook and set it on the bed beside me. It was a rough sketch of the trash can in the corner of the room, complete with overflowing beer bottles. "And try not to drink all the liquor in the city, Mr. Burnes," she said. "Your liver has to be shriveled already."

20

I needed a night out to myself, a night to enjoy a strong drink and reflect on the events at Catalina Island. My nerves were shot, and my hands were still shaking from a lack of healthy sleep. I remembered meeting a guy once at a hotel bar who wanted to quit drinking after a week-long bender. So instead of buying another bottle, he bought an eight-ball of cocaine and checked into the hotel. By the time he came down to the bar, he had torn his shirt to shreds and shaved half his head. I didn't want to be that guy. I needed a drink, fast.

I called Steve to update him on the events at Catalina. He sounded amused by the phony memorial, the gluttons on the beach, and the coolers packed with alcohol. But I knew that if our roles were reversed and he had woken up with his face in the sand, he would have had a full-fledged meltdown. I pictured him tearing off his clothes, sprinting into the ocean, and bobbing in the waves until the Coast Guard had to rescue him fifty yards offshore.

He was less amused by the snake in Jaselle's bed. "Do you think it was meant for Carter?" he asked. "Like some sort of hostile takeover of the company?"

"It's possible. These people are animals, Steven. Not a single one of them cares that Jordan was murdered."

"Careful, Billy, it's starting to sound like you feel sorry for the guy," Steve said, the hint of amusement returning to his voice.

"There's no denying that Jordan was an asshole, but these people chose to work and live with him every day. And now they're relieved that he's gone." As the words left my mouth, I thought that maybe Steve was right about my change of emotions. Maybe the lack of love for Jordan had actually compelled me to forgive his decrepit personality.

Jeez, I thought to myself, I'm getting soft.

"That's unfortunate," Steve said. "I'd be sad for at least a day if you left us."

"That warms my heart, Steven," I grumbled, unsure if he was joking or not. "But seriously, these people don't care about anything except their bank accounts. I know you had to force me to take this story, but now I want to find out who killed Jordan just to see the look on their face when they realize they've traded in their yacht club membership for lunch duty and a prison cell."

Steve chuckled. "Billy, I haven't heard you talk like this in a long time, at least back to when I thought you could be a decent journalist."

"You're full of compliments today," I growled.

"Lighten up, I'm just kidding. You're a good journalist when you follow the story and not the booze."

"I never follow the booze; it follows me."

Steve snorted. "That might be worse."

"How about we get back to psychoanalyzing Jordan?" I said. "From an outsider's perspective, it looked like he was living the dream, but I think he was lonely and trying to fill in the gaps, and it ultimately led to his death." I paused to take a breath. "That's a story worth telling."

"Yes, it is," Steve replied. "Just be careful. Watch your back around these people. If they could do that to one of their own, then they're just waiting for the right opportunity to do it to you."

I told him I'd be fine and hung up. I couldn't help but think that a lot of people had been telling me to watch my back lately.

I took a shower to rinse the sand out of my hair and then drove over the hill to Ocean Beach. There were signs for a street market on Newport Ave, where most of the bars and restaurants were clustered within a few blocks of each other. It sounded like the right atmosphere, with the right vibes I was looking for. My instincts warned me that the place would be crawling with hippies, but at this point, as long as I had a beer in my hand, I didn't care if one sat on my lap and whipped their dreadlocks in my face.

Newport Ave was closed to through traffic, so I parked a few blocks away and walked to the market. It was a beautiful day despite the onslaught of wind, and the streets were crowded with families, beach bums, and guys on skateboards. The market itself was the heart of the community. Vendors had pitched their tents on both sides of the street and in the parking lots spilling out from the road. Opportunists hoping for spare change played guitars or recited poetry on the sidewalk. A barefoot man walked down the sidewalk, stopping at stands to chat with vendors and sample their goods. His dreadlocks were pulled back, and his shirt was unbuttoned. He never bought anything at the stalls he visited, but he nodded and shared a smile with everyone he met.

The market stretched along the street almost to the ocean. At the end of the street, a patch of grass separated the pavement from the sand. A drum circle had taken over half of the grass. They beat their drums with a hypnotic rhythm and flailed their heads to the beat. A woman holding a baton danced in the middle of the circle. She tossed the baton into the air, caught it, and twirled it around her back.

Bums, smokers, and people-watchers sat on the ocean wall overlooking the beach. One lady offered me homemade beads when I sat down next to her, and her partner held up a bottle of rum, offering me a shot for a dollar. A man on roller skates glided by and blew a kiss to every woman he passed. He was old, shirtless, and in the prime of his life.

The beach was bustling with every sort of person. Children played in the surf while their fathers stood at attention. Tourists carried their shoes and walked through the sand in their socks. Half-naked sunbathers stretched out on their towels, soaking up the last hours of prime sunlight. Everyone pulsed with a rhythm that only exists when humanity is connected to the earth.

The ocean swell was wild and fierce. Surfers bobbed up and down on the waves, waiting for one that wouldn't topple them over. Further out in the ocean, sailboats dotted the horizon like they were painted on a canvas. I think I could have sat on that ocean wall forever, watching the people and the water and the sailboats. It was an endless summer that filled the soul and made the world feel like a good and happy place.

I found a bar called Jerry's around the corner from the market. Its roll-up window was open, and I could see people setting up sound equipment on the stage. A doorman sat on a stool in front of the entrance, checking IDs. He was big, shaggy, and looked like he worked for cigarette and booze money. He charged me a dollar to get in. I asked why a dollar, and he said the boss only charged a cover on market days because there was live reggae music all night, and he wanted to make sure customers had money to spend.

Inside, half the space was taken up by the stage and dance floor. There was a bar opposite the stage and a few high-top tables separating the dance floor from the drinking area. I went to the bar and ordered a whiskey. I couldn't tell if the bartender was attractive because her arms and face were almost completely covered with tattoos. But she smiled and called me "Hun" when she poured my drink. A few other lonely degenerates were already bellied up to the bar. They were the ones who showed up before the party started so they wouldn't be left out. I could relate to that crowd.

We drank peacefully until the sun set. Then the market patrons began to file in. The first to arrive were the old hippies, who wanted to feel young again. They were followed by the young hippies, who believed this was the place they had to be to remain credible. I had never been surrounded by so much long hair and dreadlocks. My gut reaction was to slip out the back door, but the whiskey was cheap, and the people were friendly. So I ordered another drink and told myself to behave.

By the time the second band had played a few songs, the alcohol and music had me feeling light and happy. I even caught myself tapping along to the reggae beat. I struck up conversation with a group of middle-aged guys wearing Grateful Dead shirts and talking like they had been at Woodstock. Normally, I would have cursed their mothers for their conception, but not tonight. Tonight, I was no longer just a professional journalist;

I was also a professional human being with the grace to accept all the hippies and degenerates just as they were.

Jewels called, and I stepped outside to answer. "Hi, babe," I said.

"Hi. How are you?" She sounded sad or tired. Or maybe both; I couldn't tell.

"I'm good," I said. "How are you?"

"I'm OK. What are you doing?"

"Sitting at a reggae bar. You'd be proud of me. I haven't told any hippies to slice their thighs and swim into the ocean."

There was a pause on the other end of the line. "What?" she replied, confused.

"Because of the sharks, you know? They're attracted to blood."

"Oh," she said and paused again. A silence rose between us. Maybe she was waiting for me to say something more, but I didn't know what to say. I was never good in these situations, and it made me sad. I suddenly wished we didn't have to talk on the phone and that she was here to share the night with me.

"I miss you," I said.

"I miss you too," she said softly. "When are you coming home?"

"I'm not sure, but I have to write this story."

"You don't have to, Billy," she said less softly. "Leave it to the police. It's their job to track down murderers."

"I can't just drop it. Steve said my job could depend on it."

"But you've been gone for weeks." Her voice grew more desperate. "You said you didn't find anything worth writing about when you were at the border. Now you're sitting at a bar, and who knows where you'll end up tonight. Stop chasing stories, Billy. It's time to come home."

"Jewels, it's not like I'm causing any trouble," I said, trying to ease her anxiety. "I'm trying to do something good here." But even to me, my defense sounded hollow and unconvincing.

"It's tough tonight, Billy." Her voice started to lose its fire. "I'm not going to lie, I think about you all day long and worry about you getting home safe, and I'm tired of worrying."

The tone of her voice made the pit of sadness in my stomach throb. "Don't worry about me," I said. "I'll be OK. I always make it home in one piece."

Jewels hesitated before sighing. "That's not the point, Billy."

I knew there was nothing left to say to make up for my absence, and it made me feel rotten. For a man who made a living with words, I didn't know how to tell her I was sorry for everything I'd put her through. I told her I loved her. She said she loved me, too, then hung up.

The night air was cool, and the wind had died down. I looked up at the stars and palm trees, then at the people passing by, and wondered if I was destined to ruin every relationship in my life. Maybe I was better off stumbling around on my own; that way, I wouldn't drag anyone else down with me. It was a dark thought on a beautiful night.

The group of middle-aged Dead Heads was walking out of Jerry's as I started back in. They each slapped the doorman on the back and laughed with him as they filed out. They saw me and asked if I wanted to smoke with them.

"Sure," I replied. "As long as it doesn't make me see a dragon or my dead grandmother walking down the street."

One of them laughed. "No way, man. It's just some grass."

"OK. I'm in," I said.

We huddled together in a circle, and one of them pulled out a pair of joints from his shirt pocket. He crouched behind the guy next to him and lit both joints. He straightened up and passed one to his right and one to his left. I watched the joints creep around each side of the circle toward me. Their ends flared bright red as the men inhaled. Smoke briefly filled the air before the wind caught it and blew it away. The joints reached me from each side at the same time.

"That's good luck, man," one of the Dead Heads said as I grabbed both joints. The others laughed and said, "Right on," and "Hell yeah."

I took a hit from each one and passed them along. The smoke immediately filled my lungs and brain. I felt myself drifting away from the group, the bar, and the ground. I floated for a couple of minutes above my body before the laughter of the Dead Heads brought me back down.

"Dude is stoned," one guy drawled, nodding toward me. "Way cool, brother," said another. They all laughed as if it were the greatest night of their lives.

We finished the joints, and the Dead Heads broke the huddle to head back inside. I thanked them for the smoke but told them I was too ripped to go back in. They shook my hand, clapped me on the back, and told me to have a great night. Then they went inside, leaving me alone again on the sidewalk.

I called for a ride back to the Swan and waited on the curb. The music from inside Jerry's spilled out to the street and kept me company. A beach kid rode by on a skateboard. He had long, blonde hair and baggy clothes. "Got any cash?" he asked as he stopped in front of me. I reached into my pocket and pulled out the only bill I had left. It was a ten-dollar bill. I handed the kid the money. "Thanks," he said and sped away to wherever beach kids go when they have spare cash.

When a car pulled in front of me, I confirmed my name with the driver and got into the back seat. He whipped away from the curb and tore through the neighborhood toward the Swan. I watched the streetlights fly by and thought about my conversation with Jewels, and it made me feel lonely again. I knew I chased stories because I thought they gave me purpose in life, but I also knew the stories were just words on paper. They were observations and narratives about other people's lives, and the whole time I was writing about someone else's life, I was forgetting about the people in my own.

I figured Jordan had gotten caught up in a similar chase. When he couldn't find the love he craved at home, he turned his attention to the bright lights he could pursue. Now, the only person who cared that he was gone was his mother, and even she had lost her relationship with her son a long time ago.

I picked up the phone to call Jewels, but then put it back down. It was late, and she was probably asleep. I told myself I would call her tomorrow and tell her I loved her.

21

The sunlight streaming through the window blinds woke me the next morning. I lay in bed for a few minutes, conducting a mental pat-down of my body for any wounds or bruises. My head was a bit groggy, but I was still in one piece and felt surprisingly fine.

Claire was working at the front desk when I made it down to the lobby. I waved and smiled at her. Her hand fluttered in something like a return wave, then she quickly looked back down at her computer. Seeing me must have brought back memories of fear and death.

I thought about calling a cab to take me back to my car, but the air was clean and the wind was gentle, so I decided to walk over the hill to Ocean Beach. By the time I reached the top of the peninsula, my shirt was soaked with sweat, and my stomach groaned. I trudged down the other side, telling myself the panoramic view of the ocean justified the walk. I stopped at a corner market advertising artisan sandwiches. The guy who made my sandwich had a pin on his shirt that read "Certified Sandwich Artist." I didn't know someone could be a sandwich artist, but he did make a good-looking sub.

I ate on a wooden bench outside the market and pulled up the website for the Carter Real Estate Company. Jordan's agent page still listed a couple of houses under his name. The houses had addresses scattered throughout the greater San Diego area, each listed for millions of dollars. I remembered Dustin taking a phone call during the poker game and telling Matt that the Topanga house was ready. Jordan's agent page listed a home at 254 Topanga Court, located in a gated community in La Jolla and priced at nearly five million dollars. I thought the price was excessive based on the thumbnails, but maybe that was by intention. An overpriced home in a gated community would attract little foot traffic from potential buyers, and less foot traffic meant more opportunities to stash drugs out of sight.

I finished my sandwich and walked the rest of the way to my car. Newport Ave was just as busy as it had been during the street market. A steady stream of cars and scooters searched for parking in front of already crowded bars and restaurants. The sidewalks buzzed with people who waved and said hello as they passed by. It was just another beautiful day in the endless string of beautiful days that is Southern California.

By early afternoon, I was pulling up to Topanga Court in La Jolla. A security gate guarded the neighborhood, so I parked down the street where any cars entering or exiting would be visible. The houses surrounding Topanga Court were smaller than those inside the gated community. They were still nice houses, probably well above my financial means, but clearly separated from the financially elite by a large iron gate and a few fewer zeros on their paychecks.

After half an hour of waiting, I began to question the effectiveness of my stakeout. Dustin had mentioned that the house would be ready on Thursday, but for all I knew, they might have already come and gone, or they might not be here for hours. This whole detective thing wasn't a good use of time, and I could understand why investigators became grumpy as they wasted away their lives waiting for others to slip up.

My phone rang; the sudden noise made me jump in my seat. It was Jewels. "Hi, babe," I whispered, then wondered why I whispered.

"Hi," she said cautiously. "Why are you whispering?"

"Sorry," I said a little too loudly. "I didn't mean to whisper; everything is fine. How are you?"

"Um, I'm good." She paused. "I wanted to apologize for last night. I know you're working and—"

"Julianna," I interrupted. "I should be the one apologizing. I know I've been gone too long. I just need to finish up here, and I'll be home, I promise."

Jewels was silent on the other end of the line. She probably didn't know how to respond to my apology since I rarely took responsibility for the damage I caused to our relationship. She was about to say something else when Matt's Bronco drove past my jeep.

"Oh shit," I whispered, throwing my seat back and spilling my drink in my lap. I grabbed the cup but had nothing to wipe the wetness now covering the front of my jeans.

"Billy, what happened?" Jewels asked.

"Jewels, I have to go," I whispered.

"Is everything OK?" Her voice carried a renewed sense of alarm.

"Yes. I'm sorry, I just have to go." I hung up and slid lower in the seat.

I recognized Dustin's bald head sitting in the passenger seat of the Bronco. A white maintenance van followed closely behind, with two people I didn't recognize sitting in the cab. Both vehicles stopped in front of the gate, and Matt leaned out of the Bronco to punch in the passcode. The gate opened, and both vehicles drove through.

What appeared to be a normal, everyday event screamed suspicion to me. A maintenance van pulling up to a house for sale in the middle of the afternoon would be a subtle way to transport drug shipments. Neighbors wouldn't even look twice at the boxes being loaded and unloaded, or at the people coming and going from the vacant home.

I remained parked down the street and weighed my options. I could wait for another car to open the gate, then drive in, snap a few pictures, and inform Detective Pratt of my theory. But the police would need more than just a maintenance van and testimony from a guy at a bar. They'd probably stake out the house, just like I was doing now, and run me out of the neighborhood. Besides, it wouldn't make for a good story. No one wants to read about the cops unless they're doing something criminal. I decided my best move was to continue investigating on my own.

I moved my jeep to the other side of the street and waited. Twenty minutes later, the Bronco came back through the gate. I hunched down in case Dustin or Matt looked my way, but the Bronco turned in the opposite direction and kept driving. The maintenance van followed closely behind again, but this time there was only one person in the cab.

I waited until the Bronco and maintenance van disappeared around the corner before hitting the gas. The gate's automated sensors kicked it back open, and I drove through slowly to avoid drawing attention. Wealthy people are always on the lookout for anything or anyone out of place. The last thing I wanted was a security guard escorting me out of the neighborhood and possibly alerting whoever was inside the house.

The houses lining the street were massive, with lawns that were perfectly manicured. The only person in sight was a lone gardener trimming the shrubs in front of a white stucco house. He didn't look up as I drove past. The neighborhood reminded me of a book I read as a kid, in which the main characters travel to an alternate dimension where everything looked the same and moved at the same cadence. The book freaked me out as a kid, and I felt the same way now as I drove deeper into the neighborhood.

I found the house from Jordan's listing, parked a little further down the street, and then walked back. The house was two stories with a white exterior and red clay shingles. There was a for-sale sign in the front yard, the blinds were drawn, and the patio was empty. It was an oversized shell of a home, devoid of life or personal character.

I pulled out my phone and snapped a picture, then just stood there, unsure what to do next. Should I knock and feign interest in buying the house? Or maybe pretend to be a salesman selling home security systems? Neither option seemed convincing, and the chances of anyone answering the door and inviting me inside for a tour were nonexistent. To hell with it, I thought, I'll just wing it.

My knuckles rapping on the front door sounded like knocking on the walls of a giant cave. I imagined the echo bouncing down every hallway and through every empty room. I leaned forward and pressed my ear to the door, but didn't hear any sounds of movement or anyone inside. In fact, the entire street was silent. There were no people out walking, no birds chirping, and no dogs barking. The loudest thing was my heartbeat pounding in my chest.

I walked past the garage to the side gate, where three trash cans were lined up along the driveway. Maybe I could use a trash can to hop the gate, take pictures of any evidence in the backyard, and get out before anyone knew I was there. I gave one of the trash cans a little tug. It felt sturdy enough to support my weight. So I pulled it over to the gate and put both hands on the lid to push myself up, but then I stopped.

Was I really about to do this? Breaking and entering into any house, let alone a possible stash house, could land me in jail or worse. I thought about the woman from the border whose son had been killed by the cartels and about Jordan lying on the pool deck with a sword through his back. Both stories served as warnings about how far evil people would go to hold onto their power. Hopping the gate in front of me meant I, too, might become a warning to others.

But then I thought about Jewels. I talked a big game to her, but she knew her worthless boyfriend was just a self-centered, drunk blowhard. She had no reason to believe otherwise. I also thought about Steve and my track record at the office. My failure at the border was just another failure in a growing list of missed opportunities and broken promises.

I was tired of lying to myself and everyone around me.

So I put my hands back on the lid, pushed my stomach and legs onto the can, and stood up like an amateur surfer about to face plant in the waves. I paused for a second to steady myself and then climbed over the gate. The sound of my shoes hitting the concrete echoed along the side of the house. I crouched down, half expecting a guard dog to come howling around the corner, but nothing happened.

I took one step, then another, and then hugged the wall as I crept along the walkway. It might have been my imagination, but it suddenly felt much hotter outside. My forehead was covered in sweat after just a few steps. I looked back at the gate and realized I hadn't thought of a way to get over from this side. I wiped the sweat from my eyes and cursed myself for my reckless choices.

To my left was a door leading into the garage. To my right was a ten-foot-high stucco wall separating the property from the neighbor. Tools and debris were scattered at the base of the wall, presumably from a remodeling project, which would be another perfect excuse to delay the sale of the home. It would also provide cover for supposed construction workers coming and going. Jordan and his accomplices could hide in plain sight while they moved their shipments in and out of the house.

I reached the end of the walkway and peeked around the corner. The backyard was smaller than I had expected. A raised patio deck and a narrow lap pool took up most of the space. There was a small lawn behind the pool and a flower bed along the back wall, but the whole yard felt cramped considering the neighborhood's wealth and the home's inflated listing price.

Just as I was about to turn the corner, a sliding door opened on the patio. I flinched back behind the corner, pressed myself flat against the house, and held my breath. The gate I had hopped over just a minute ago suddenly seemed very far away, and I hoped whoever had come out to the patio was blind, deaf, or crippled. But as these thoughts somersaulted through my head, the sliding door closed again. I waited another full minute before exhaling, then dared another peek around the corner. The backyard was empty and silent.

A rational person would have turned around at this point. After all, I was just an investigative journalist, not a seasoned detective or a ferocious fighter. I wielded a pen and a laptop, striking from the safety of my office. But here I was now, in the belly of the beast with no backup or escape plan.

I took a breath to calm my nerves and stepped out of my hiding spot. Hugging the side of the house, I inched my way to the patio and crept up a small set of wooden steps. I stopped short of the sliding glass door and tried to peer through, but the reflection from the sun obscured my view into the house. I cupped my hands around my face and pressed my forehead against the glass. The inside of the house appeared empty of furniture and people.

The door slid easily when I tested the handle. I opened it a little more and waited. When there was no sound from inside the house, I continued sliding the door as smoothly as possible. It was halfway open when another door inside the house opened and closed. My body stiffened. A man appeared around a corner, and I ducked away from the sliding door, praying I had moved fast enough.

"Aye," the man shouted, and I started to run.

The sliding door yanked open, and footsteps chased after me. I turned the corner of the house and crashed into a pile of debris, sending tools and nails skidding across the pathway. I took off again at a sprint toward the gate and tried to push it open, but it only rattled under my frantic shoves.

Footsteps pounded on the pavement behind me. I turned and raised my arms as the first punch sailed toward my head. It glanced off my arms but pushed me back into the gate. The next punches came frantically, and I covered my head and tried bobbing to dodge the blows. Then the man stopped throwing punches and took a step back. When I looked up to see what he was doing, his knee shot up under my arms and into my stomach. The air rushed from my lungs as my knees hit the concrete. Then his fist came down heavy on my head, and everything went black.

When I regained consciousness, the man was dragging me on my back across the concrete. He had a hold of both my ankles and was tugging my weight in short heaves. He wasn't a large man, but he tugged with purpose. I reached out to grasp hold of anything I could, but my body felt disconnected from my brain, and my fingers brushed uselessly along the property wall.

The man saw my pointless flailing. He let go of one of my legs and lunged at my head. His fist connected with my jaw, and the world exploded in black dots.

I woke up again when the man picked me up and shoved me into a chair. It took a moment for my vision to clear and for me to realize we were in the garage. The man hadn't noticed that I was awake this time, so I let my shoulders slump forward and dropped my head to pretend I was still unconscious.

The man stepped back and said something in Spanish. A few seconds later, he was arguing with someone in aggressive whispers. I lifted my head an inch and cracked open one eye. The man was talking on the phone and pacing back and forth across the garage. A floodlight in the corner outlined his shape like some sort of ghostly figure.

My arms hung loosely at my sides, and I wiggled my fingers to check if the feeling had returned. I tilted my chin side to side to get a sense of my surroundings while keeping an eye on the man who was speaking in increasingly harsh tones. Next to me was a table with tools spread across it and some boxes stacked underneath. There was also a set of shelves along one wall that held more boxes.

I closed my eyes again when the man stopped talking. His footsteps stomped toward me, and he grabbed my shoulders and pushed me back against the chair. As he did, I kicked as hard as I could, hitting him between the legs. The man doubled over and staggered backward. I grabbed the handle of something hard off the table and swung it at his head. The sound of metal hitting bone would have been sickening under any other circumstance. The man shrieked and collapsed to the floor. I looked down and realized I was holding something that looked like a meat tenderizer.

I stood up and stepped toward the door, but the world spun, and I dropped to my knees. The tenderizer slipped from my hand and slid across the floor. I tried to stand back up but stumbled again. By then, the man had raised himself to one knee and was holding the side of his face. Blood dripped down his cheek and into his mouth, filling the gaps between his teeth. He rose with a guttural scream that could only be conjured by a demon and started toward me again.

The adrenaline surging through my veins was enough to pick me up this time and carry me toward the door. I tumbled through it and was momentarily stunned to find myself inside the house. The natural light stung my eyes, but I stumbled further into the house, searching for a way out. As I crashed into the island in the kitchen, the man grabbed the back of my shirt. I spun around and threw a haymaker, landing it on the side of his head. The man shuffled backward, and I thought about hitting him again, but decided to take advantage of the space between us and continued running.

A sliding glass door appeared in the middle of a sitting room, and I hurried toward it, not considering the possibility of getting trapped in the backyard. The only thought in my mind was that sunlight meant freedom. But when I stepped outside, I found myself in a courtyard enclosed by glass walls and filled with gravel pathways and miniature trees. I ran to the center of the courtyard, trying to locate another exit, and then realized the man hadn't followed me outside. I spun around in a circle, trying to see him through the glass walls, but I couldn't find him.

I pulled my phone out of my pocket, dialed 9-1, then hung up before finishing. The cops wouldn't arrive in time if the man decided to come out of hiding, and if he heard the sound of approaching sirens, he might be forced to take more drastic measures. I put my phone back in my pocket, found another sliding glass door, and hurried back inside.

The house was quiet again. There was no heavy breathing around the corner; no feet stomping down the hallway. I crept through what might have been a living room and finally spotted the front door. I started toward it, but stopped when I noticed a trail of blood on the carpet leading to the entryway and up the stairs.

"You only need to be faster than him," I told myself, then I sprinted toward freedom.

The moment my feet made noise, a growl came from the stairs, and the man flew over the banister. I lowered my shoulder and slammed into his chest. Had he been a bigger man or able to plant his feet, my charge would have been a foolish move. But my momentum sent him crashing into the wall behind him and knocked me to the floor. I pushed myself up and ran to him before he could get back on his feet. My fist connected with his chin while he was still on his hands and knees. He dropped to the floor and grabbed at my ankles, but there was no real strength left in his hands, and I kicked them away. I reached the front door, fumbled with the deadbolt until it unlocked, and burst out into the afternoon light.

I sprinted to my car and jumped in; only then did I look back. The man hadn't followed me outside. Silence gripped the neighborhood like an episode of *The Twilight Zone*; nothing

174

moved or made a sound. The front door of the house was
closed as I drove past.

22

I drove back to the Swan with shaking hands and blood pulsing in my ears. I picked up the phone twice to call Detective Pratt but decided against it both times. If the police found out I had trespassed on a point of interest, they would surely bar me from further investigation. But this was my story to tell. My job and livelihood depended on it.

On the hundredth time checking the rearview mirror, I was finally convinced no one was following me. When I arrived at the Swan, I hurried to my room to avoid any uncomfortable questions from patrons and employees in the lobby. I threw my keys on the bed and went to the bathroom. There was a nasty cut above my eye and dried blood on my nose. If my face didn't hurt so badly, I would have thought it was a zombie looking back at me in the mirror.

I used a washcloth to scrub the blood off my face, talking to myself as I scrubbed because the sound of silence terrorized my spooked nerves. The guy at the house would probably report to his superiors that someone had broken in, but they wouldn't know who I was or why I was there. All I had to do was stay away from the house for a few days, and everything would be fine. They would probably assume I'd call the cops, and they'd be too busy clearing the home of evidence to track me down. I told myself these things and tried to believe them.

I called Steve to tell him about the stash house. He answered the phone like he was ready to chuck it against the wall. I always told him that if he didn't get a grip on his nerves, he would die young and lonely, and I wouldn't have anything pleasant to say about him at his funeral. That would only make him more agitated. His face would turn bright red, and he would chase me out of the office with a chair raised above his head. But this time, I was the one with the severed nerves and elevated blood pressure. I told him about breaking into the house and my narrow escape. He breathed heavily into the phone while I spoke.

"Jesus," he said. "Not even a piece of shit like you deserves that sort of treatment."

"Why, thank you for your sentiment, Steven." I wasn't sure whether to laugh or sneer at him.

"Are you OK?" he asked.

"I got a pretty nasty cut above my eye, maybe a concussion, and my hands won't stop shaking. But nothing serious."

"Did you call the police?"

"Nope."

"Why not?"

Someone in the background yelled at Steve before I could reply to his question. The only person who spoke to Steve that way was our boss, Corbin.

"Corbin wants to talk to you, Billy," Steve warned. "Try to act sober."

There was some shuffling and cursing before Corbin's voice replaced Steve's. "Billy!" he shouted. "Do you really expect to have a job when you get back? I didn't think you were that psychotic. But you must be drowning in booze if you think I'm going to pay you another penny."

"Sorry, Corbin," I stammered. "I'm doing the best I can to get this new story. I think it could be a big one."

"Yes, Steve told me about it, but why the hell should I believe you'll come back with a story? You botched the border story and wasted my money, and now I'm hearing that you're going to the police with this new story. That will definitely blow up your coverage."

"Hold on. I never said I was going to the police."

"Good. Because if you go to the police and we lose this story to the rest of those goddamn leeching news outlets, then don't even think about showing your face here again."

I believed Corbin's threats, but I also knew I was lucky to escape the stash house with my life and vital organs intact. "Listen, Corbin, I'm trying. I promise. But this runs deep, maybe even to the cartels. In fact, I may have just run into one of them, and he left some pretty good marks on my face. I don't know if I'm cut out to investigate something like this."

"You better get on the fucking horse and figure out how to cover it," Corbin demanded. "I don't care what the hell you have to do or what happens to you. I hate to admit this, and I can't believe I'm in this fucking position, but *The Independent* needs this story. We have enough funding for one, maybe two more editions. If we don't get more readership soon, we'll all be living in tents."

Corbin's words surprised me. It was the most vulnerable I'd ever heard him sound. He must have really felt the noose tightening. "OK," I said after a few seconds. "I'll get the story."

"You're damn right you will."

"But Corbin, there had better be a bottle of your finest whiskey sitting on my desk when I get home."

"Sweet fucking baby..." he stopped short of saying something blasphemous. Then he hollered to Steve that he couldn't talk to me anymore.

"Why do you do that, Billy?" Steven asked when he took the phone back.

"Someone has to get him riled up," I said. "Corbin can't live right unless he's standing on the ledge."

"Our financial situation is taking care of that itself. I don't know what he'll do if he doesn't have this newspaper."

"Do we really only have two more months before we go under?"

"That's what it looks like."

"Jeez. Melissa won't like that."

"You really are a piece of shit, Billy."

"I try."

"Just get the story and get back here."

Something tingled inside me. If I wasn't mistaken, it might have been a sense of responsibility. It was a new emotion that I'd have to test out and explore. "I will," I said.

Steve paused for a moment. "And Billy, keep watching your back," he said and hung up.

I checked myself for any more injuries and then got in the shower. As the water washed away the rest of the blood from my face, I reminded myself that I was fighting the good fight and that the good guy always wins. I told myself this was the perfect opportunity to jumpstart my career and that the cut above my eye was the selling point readers would love.

It's amazing what you can delude yourself of when there's no one around to talk you down. By the time the water ran cold, I felt like a new man. It was only late afternoon, and Kylie had told me to stop by her apartment before she went out partying with her friends. I looked at my reflection one last time before leaving the room. I thought I looked pretty good for a banged-up writer with a shriveled liver.

23

Kylie's apartment was located in the Hillcrest neighborhood. The bars and coffee shops along the main road were bright, colorful, and full of life. The people walking on the streets wore a peculiar fashion I would never have the confidence to wear. Everyone had a smile on their face and a bounce in their step, as if they were happy just to be alive. The air held a refreshing youthfulness that eased the pain in my face as I drove through the neighborhood with the windows rolled down.

I pulled up to her apartment as the sun was setting. It was a small, two-story building with a courtyard and a fire pit out front. It had a homely feeling that I hadn't expected from Kylie's demeanor and choice of profession. She told me her unit was on the second floor at the end. There was a small table and two chairs in the hallway in front of her window. I knocked on the door and waited.

"Hello, detective," she said, smiling as she opened the door. She was wearing a pink and green kimono that hugged her figure and barely covered her upper thighs.

I made sure to maintain eye contact with her. "Hello, Kylie. Thank you for your offer to continue talking to me."

"Of course." She stepped back from the door to invite me in. "That looks like a nasty cut above your eye. Did you get it on Catalina?"

"I got it a few hours ago, actually," I replied, stepping into the apartment and shutting the door behind me. "But it's just a paper cut."

The living room of her apartment was fair-sized, with big windows and lots of natural light. The sense of space was amplified by the lack of furniture. There was a couch and a TV, but that was all—no coffee table in front of the TV, no blankets on the couch, and no DVDs on the TV stand. In fact, there were none of the small items people usually collect and hoard in life. I wondered if she actually spent any time here.

"Can I get you anything to drink?" she asked. "I have vodka." She started to walk to the kitchen.

Vodka sounded great, maybe even a whole bottle, but I had a job to do and a new responsibility to uphold. "Thank you," I said. "But I'll have to pass on the vodka tonight. My editor says I drink too much."

Kylie laughed. "My mom tells me the same thing. But she drinks more wine than anyone I know. It's funny how the ones who tell you to stop are usually the ones with the problem." Her words were deep and knowing. I was surprised again by her level of insight into the human psyche. "I'm just getting ready to go out tonight," she continued. "Do you mind if we talk while I finish up?"

"I don't mind."

"Good. I usually get ready in my room if you want to come in." She didn't wait for a reply and left me standing in the middle of the room. I looked around again at the emptiness of the apartment. There were no shelves with pictures or artwork hanging on the walls. The room made me feel hollow and sad.

I followed her into the bedroom and found where she lived. The entire room was filled with color, clothes, and makeup. Every inch of wall space was covered with a photograph or poster. Clothes were thrown haphazardly on the bed, and a stack of magazines sat on the nightstand with a box of chocolates on top. The TV on the dresser was playing an episode of The Real Housewives.

Kylie sat down cross-legged on the floor in front of a full-length mirror. She leaned forward and dabbed something on her face. I tried not to look at her thighs exposed below her kimono and kept myself busy searching for somewhere to stand.

"You can move the clothes and sit on the bed if you'd like," Kylie said, without pausing whatever she was putting on her face.

I moved some pants and T-shirts aside and sat down on the edge of the bed. She didn't look at me in the mirror while I moved her clothes. She didn't seem to mind that I was in her sanctuary, touching her clothes, or that she was barely dressed.

"Big plans for the night?" I asked awkwardly.

"Just meeting the girls for a little night out," she replied, not awkwardly at all. "It's been a wild couple of days. I need to let my hair down, ya know? Just relax and have a good night."

"When you say relax, you mean going out to party?"

She paused her makeup application for a moment and looked at herself in the mirror. I figured she liked what she saw, but she wasn't afraid of a little self-evaluation. "I guess it does for me," she responded with a shrug.

"Did you and Jordan go out often?"

"Sometimes. We did when we first started dating. Jordan liked to show me off. He would take me to all his parties and to Catalina for a weekend." She paused to focus on the line she was drawing above her eye. "But not so much lately," she said once she leaned back to examine her work in the mirror.

"What changed?"

"I'm not sure. Maybe he got bored of me." She didn't sound too upset if that was true, but I found it hard to believe.

"It didn't bother you that he stopped taking you out? I'm sure plenty of other guys would have jumped at the chance."

She looked at me in the mirror and smiled. "You're sweet. But no, it didn't bother me. I mean, don't get me wrong, I liked the attention, and Jordan always made the night exciting, but I like my independence too."

I took a moment to look around the room again when she went back to her makeup. There was a framed picture of her and Jordan on the dresser. There were lots of pictures of Kylie posing by herself in front of the ocean. "Did Jordan have a typical group of friends he went out with?" I asked.

"Just the guys in the office," Kylie answered. "Jordan didn't really have any friends besides them."

"Why was that?"

"Jordan was loud. He liked to be the center of attention. I think the guys in the office accepted that and knew how to handle it. I don't think other people do... did, I mean."

She tilted her face from side to side to check if her makeup was even. She looked good, but she also looked good without makeup. She stood up and straightened her kimono as if she was planning to go out in it. I caught myself staring at her reflection and looked down at the floor.

"OK," I said, looking at the carpet beneath my feet. "So he still liked to go out and party, but he wouldn't ask you to go with him? I'm not gonna lie, I don't see how he could get bored of you."

Kylie laughed. "Well, thank you, Billy. I agree." She laughed again. "I think he was putting on a show at first, like trying to impress me and show off to everyone else that he had a girl-friend. But then he stopped asking me to go out. We actually rarely saw each other."

"Did you still want to see him?"

"Of course, I did. But I'm not the type to wait around all night. This apartment gets lonely."

"Could he have been seeing someone else?" I hoped the question wasn't disrespectful, but it had to be asked.

Kylie looked at me in the mirror for a second, then answered bluntly, "Yes." She walked over to the closet and came back with a black minidress to hold up in front of the mirror. Her honesty was disarming; her lack of emotion was unsettling.

"Yes, because he stopped taking you out?" I asked. "Or was there something more?"

"Man, you really know how to drill the questions, don't you, Billy?" she said, but her voice still showed no sign of irritation. She actually seemed to be enjoying the questions.

"Sorry. I know it was an insensitive question, but it might be helpful information."

"It's OK," she said, swaying the dress as if imagining herself dancing in it. "I like people who are truthful and upfront. I meet people all day long who smile and lie to my face. It's nice to talk to someone who doesn't have ulterior motives."

"I could say the same thing about you," I said, and it was true. I always thought influencers were fake people, and that the facades they put online reflected superficial personali-ties. But Kylie seemed to be an open book. She didn't seem ashamed to show who she truly was when there wasn't a phone pointed in her direction.

She went back to the closet and picked out a different black dress. This one was a bit looser, with white ruffles at the hem and a plunging neckline. She held it up in front of the mirror and did another little dance.

I tried to steer the conversation back on track. "Did you have any ideas or suspicions about who else Jordan could have been seeing?"

"No. And that's what made me suspicious, actually. He'd say he was meeting the guys on a Friday night but wouldn't have any stories to tell the next day, and he'd never post anything about it, either."

"Maybe he just didn't post them," I said.

Kylie shot me a sarcastic look over her shoulder. "No way. Jordan always posted his whole life for everyone to see. At least all the good parts. So when it kept happening, I started to think he was trying to hide something."

"How long had this been going on?"

"For a couple of months. Only on Fridays, but not every Friday—like every other one."

"Did you ask him about it?"

"Yes, once. But he got angry and started shouting that if I couldn't trust him, I should just leave. Then we went to the bar, and I never asked him about it again. But my feelings didn't go away, and he never said anything to make me feel otherwise."

She walked to the bathroom and pushed the door shut, but it didn't close all the way. I resisted the urge to peek through the crack. I sat on the bed, waiting for her to change, and looked around the room and at the ceiling.

She came out wearing the second black dress, the one with the ruffles and plunging neckline. "How do I look?" she asked, striking a few small poses.

"Like anyone would be lucky to go out with you on a Friday night," I replied.

She laughed and smiled at me. "You are too sweet, Billy."

There was a moment of awkward silence as I imagined what it would be like to go out with her, and she knew what I was imagining. She broke the silence. "Are you going to ask me any more questions, detective?"

"I'm not sure," I stammered, then paused to collect myself. "So you really have no idea who he was seeing?"

Kylie shook her head. "No idea. I thought about following him one night, but then I thought about how crazy that would make me, and I realized I didn't really care where he went or what he was doing."

It seemed like a horrible relationship. Even the chaos I brought into my relationship with Jewels felt like it was better. "Why stay together then?"

Kylie thought about the question for a moment. "It can be tough out there for a single girl. Technically, I had a boyfriend, but I also had freedom. That made for the best of both worlds."

"And Jordan didn't care what you did with that freedom?"

"He only cared about what I was doing when he wanted to hang out. But if he didn't want to hang out, then he couldn't care less."

"I still don't understand why you wouldn't find a better boyfriend. I'm sure it wouldn't be hard."

"Oh, it wouldn't be hard," she laughed. "But Jordan had connections and helped me grow my business. So it benefited me even though he wasn't there emotionally. And the way I see it, I have the rest of my life to find someone I connect with emotionally."

"Don't wait too long," I said. "Speaking from experience."

She looked at me with evaluating eyes. Her stare had a way of capturing everything about you at once and holding you tightly before letting go. It was both unnerving and intoxicating. "Do you want to go out with us tonight, Billy?" she asked.

"I'd love to, but I have someone at home who probably wouldn't be happy about it, and I'm trying to be a better boyfriend."

Kylie smiled, and her gaze released me. "She is a lucky lady."

"I've put her through hell many times. Honestly, I don't understand why she's still with me."

"Do you love her?"

"Yes."

"Does she love you?"

"I hope so. I think so."

"Then you guys will be OK."

Her phone buzzed on the bedside table, and she moved next to me to pick it up. Her perfume filled my nose and my mind. "My ride's here," she said.

"Time to party?" I asked.

"Time to party," she replied.

She finally stepped away from the bed after what felt like forever and grabbed her purse hanging on the bedroom door. She took one last look in the mirror, pulled her dress down a bit to show more cleavage, and smiled to let me know she was ready.

"Thank you for talking to me tonight, Kylie. It was very helpful," I said, standing up from the bed.

"I hope you find out who killed Jordan," she said casually, as if she were talking about the weather. "He could be an asshole, but no one deserves to be stabbed in the back."

I followed her to the front door and waited outside while she locked up. We walked down the stairs to the street and to a black SUV waiting for her in the middle of the road. The back window rolled down, and a young blonde girl leaned out and yelled to Kylie. Kylie waved and yelled back.

Then she turned to me. "I hope you and your girlfriend are happy, Billy. You can call me anytime."

I opened the back door for her, and we were met with a chorus of cheers from Kylie's girlfriends. The driver also turned around to greet her, and I realized it was Charlie. His eyes bulged when he saw me, and he jerked back around. I closed the door, and the SUV drove away. This time, I was the one left alone on the sidewalk in this big, scary world. I watched the SUV go with a lonely feeling in my heart.

24

I was surprised to find Carter and Jaselle at the Blue Swan when I returned to the motel. They were sitting by themselves at the bar. Carter had a full drink in his hand and was staring at the wall behind the bar. Jaselle's drink was sitting on the bar in front of her. She was slowly swirling it with a straw and gazing into its liquid depths.

"Good evening, Carter," I said as I approached from behind. "I'm surprised to see you here tonight."

Carter slowly turned at the sound of his name. His eyes were vacant. "I'm surprised to be here myself," he responded.

"Are you guys meeting anyone tonight?"

Carter shook his head. "It's just the two of us and a ghost."

I thought it might be in poor taste to interrupt a man in mourning, but I was tired and needed a drink. "Mind if I join the party?" I asked.

"Please do." He waved a hand at the chair beside him. "Once Tim makes you a few drinks, you'll be talking to everyone you've ever known."

I nodded like I understood, even though I questioned the sanity of a man who believed alcohol consumption could revive the dead. It appeared Tim had already made Carter more than a few drinks.

I waved to Jaselle before sitting down. "Hi, Jaselle. I hope your evening is going well."

Jaselle's lips were as bright red as ever, but her eyes held little light. She looked exhausted, as if she had lived a whole lifetime in just a few short years. She absentmindedly stirred her drink and tried to smile. "Hello, Billy. It's a fine night," she said softly. "It's nice to see you."

I figured both of her statements were lies.

I made eye contact with Tim, and he hurried over. "Good evening, Billy," he said, and grabbed a bottle of whiskey before I could reply. "Whiskey neat for you tonight?"

"Good evening, Tim. That's the magic, thank you." As the words left my mouth, I realized only alcoholics and college kids call alcohol magic, and I was too old to be a college kid.

Tim poured my drink to the top of the glass and said the first one was on the house. I thanked him again and raised my glass to Carter and Jaselle. Carter raised his glass in return.

"What brings you here tonight, Carter?" I asked after we both had sipped from our drinks. "If you don't mind my asking."

Carter didn't answer right away. He took another sip and returned his stare to the wall behind the bar. Maybe that's where his alcohol-fueled portal to the afterlife was. "I thought I'd feel something coming back here," he said after choosing his words carefully. "It sounds weird to say out loud, but I thought Jordan's presence would be here."

It was an honest answer from a hard man.

"Do you feel anything?" I asked.

"I don't know," he answered. "It's just a sea of memories."

"Happy ones, hopefully?"

Carter finished his drink and set the glass on the bar. He signaled to Tim, who hurried over and refilled the glass without further prompting. Carter waited until Tim walked away before speaking again.

"When Jordan was six, he wanted a dog. He begged his mother and me every day to get him one. So on his seventh birthday, I surprised him by taking him to a breeder, and I told him to pick out his favorite one. He must have looked at every dog ten times; he couldn't make up his mind. Finally, he picked the biggest one. He said it would grow up to be the strongest of the litter. But a year later, Jordan hardly acknowledged the dog's existence. He wouldn't play with it, feed it, or clean up after it. I tried to force him to play with the dog, but Jordan just didn't care; he said he would rather play with his friends. So, I gave the dog away to a family I'd sold a house to. They had a couple of kids and seemed like a happy family."

I waited for Carter to finish the story, but he didn't say anything more. "What did Jordan say when he found out you gave his dog away?"

"He asked what happened to it a few days later when he realized it wasn't around. He wasn't upset, though, and he never mentioned the dog again."

I thought it was a miserable story. It was my turn to empty my glass, and I called Tim over for another. Carter stood up from his stool and said he was going to light a cigar by the pool. I asked him if he wanted some company, but he said he needed a few minutes of solitude and reflection. He didn't say anything to Jaselle as he walked out.

Jaselle and I remained at the bar in awkward silence. She hadn't spoken since we exchanged hellos, nor had she looked up from her drink, which she was still absentmindedly stirring. Maybe she was thinking about the series of life choices that brought her to this barstool at this moment in time. Maybe she was trying to create a whirlpool that would pull her in and carry her away from this place.

"Were you and Jordan close, Jaselle?" I asked.

Jaselle flinched at the sound of my voice. "A little," she mumbled.

"How long had you known him?" I asked, hoping the question sounded like polite conversation. Jaselle's fragile mood couldn't handle too much more pressure.

"For as long as I've known Ross," she answered.

"How long would that be?"

"We've been married for three years. We met just a few months before getting married. So, it's been about three years and a few months, I guess."

"I'm sorry again for your loss," I said, but the words sounded cheap.

"Thank you, Billy." She stopped stirring her drink and waited for the liquid to settle, then took a small sip. Her lips were such a bright red that it was hard not to stare at them while she drank. They left a red smudge on the rim of the glass.

"How did you and Carter meet?"

She started stirring her glass again before responding. "We were at a party at a mutual friend's house. Ross said he saw me from across the room and knew we'd get married."

"Sounds like a fairy tale."

She looked at me again with those eyes that had lived someone else's life for too long. "Maybe it was," she said softly.

"Is it still?"

She hesitated. "That's a very personal question, Billy." Her tone and slow response answered my question.

"I'm sorry," I said. "A lot of people have been telling me that lately."

Jaselle rested her chin on her shoulder and peered out at Carter. I followed her gaze. Carter was sitting in a lounge chair by the pool, holding a cigar in one hand and a glass in the other. The patio lights above the pool cast shadows across his face. The red glow from the tip of his cigar hovered in the air around him like a satanic firefly.

Jaselle turned back to the bar, took a breath, and decided to continue. "Ross likes to be in control. I think that was part of his attraction in the beginning. But it can wear on a person."

"That makes sense," I said.

She paused again, and I felt sorry for her despite her fairy-tale marriage, wealth, and status. She was just a girl trapped in a life that had swept her up too fast. She never took the time or made the effort to discover who she truly was. Now, she was a trophy wife on the arm of an older man and expected to play the part.

"How did Jordan react to your marriage?" I asked. "I imagine he must have had mixed feelings about having a stepmother your age."

Jaselle took a long sip of her drink. When she set the glass down again, she exhaled slowly. "Honestly, Jordan didn't seem to care at first. He was only focused on building his career. I don't think he cared what his father did outside of the company."

"Things changed, though?"

Her sad eyes somehow grew even sadder. "Things always change, Billy."

Carter's voice rang out behind us and snapped us back to the present. "Am I interrupting anything?" he asked. He looked at Jaselle, then at me, and then back to Jaselle. A slight smile crept onto his face.

Jaselle didn't respond and went back to stirring her drink. Carter sat down between us, calm and at ease.

"I was just asking Jaselle how you two met," I said.

"Aw. I believe it was at a party, right, Jazz?" He looked at Jaselle, who didn't answer."Jazz, tell us about the party," Carter continued.

Jaselle suddenly stopped stirring her drink and turned to face Carter. "Will you please just fucking stop? Please. Just stop this." There were tears in her eyes, but there was also anger in her voice.

Carter didn't flinch. He was about to say something more when the lobby door swung open and Dustin stepped inside. He stopped when he saw us sitting at the bar, and his face twisted with either surprise or anger. Carter saw him too.

"What the hell are you doing here?" Carter growled. His voice could have frozen a bonfire. He spoke loudly enough for the entire restaurant to hear, and it may have been my imagination, but everyone and everything around us stopped what they were doing.

"I didn't expect to see you here, Carter," Dustin said, then he pointed at me. "I came for him."

I wasn't surprised to see his finger outstretched in my direction. I had tried to convince myself that my intrusion into the house on Topanga Court would be forgotten, but reality and retribution aren't that kind.

Carter spoke before I could acknowledge Dustin's gesture. "I don't care who you came for. You should turn around and leave before this gets ugly."

Dustin ignored the advice. He took a few steps toward the bar but still kept a safe distance from Carter. "Don't be angry at me, Carter. Jordan knew what he was getting into."

"You corrupted him, though," Carter growled. "You were the one to whisper in his ear, to make him want more than he could hold."

"Come on, Carter. Be real," Dustin scoffed. "You know better than anyone that Jordan was blinded by ambition. Someone was bound to get him eventually."

Carter slammed his hand on the bar. "I gave you and everyone else at the company everything you ever needed. I made you wealthy. I made you important. But that wasn't enough for you, you son of a bitch."

"You can't speak to me like that, Carter," Dustin growled back. His anger and backbone were strengthening as the exchange went on.

Carter rose from his stool. He was a big man, and even with a gut full of liquor, he would have been a bear to handle physically. "I'll speak however I goddamn please. Now you can leave on your own, or we can both go outside and see what happens."

Dustin's face scrunched up in his trademark smashed-Mr. -Potato-Head look. "Fine. I have nothing more to say to you, Carter." Then he looked at me and jabbed his finger again in my direction. "But you, Billy. You have no idea who you are messing with. Things will get very bad for you if you keep showing up where you're not supposed to."

I usually wouldn't pay much attention to verbal threats hurled my way; I'd heard all sorts of them in my time. But I had just received a very real taste of what Dustin's cohorts were capable of. They were not the type of people to toss around empty threats, nor were they bound by laws or morals. I figured my safest option at the moment was to act naive and hope the danger would pass.

"I'm not sure what you're talking about, Dustin," I said, trying to sound more confident than I felt.

"I think you do. Don't play dumb. If you keep coming around, someone's eventually going to cut you up." He paused, and his eyes tried to bore two holes through me. "And don't expect the police to offer enough protection. They won't. And they can't."

"I don't have any need for the police," I said. "And I'll go wherever I want to." The words came out on their own, and I felt a brief flash of pride.

Dustin didn't seem to appreciate my pride. "I suggest you go back to whatever shithole you climbed out of," he said.

Carter shifted his weight as if he were preparing to lunge forward. Dustin noticed his movement and shuffled back a few inches.

"The same can be said of you, Dustin," Carter said. "Now, get the hell out of here."

Dustin looked at us. We looked back at Dustin. The rest of the bar watched all three of us. It was a scene worthy of a movie showdown.

Finally, Dustin raised both hands in the air. "Have it your way, gentlemen," he said. "But you've been warned." He took a step back and waited to see if Carter would follow. When Carter didn't move, Dustin turned on his heel and walked out of the lobby. He marched to his car, opened the door, and paused to look back at us once more through the lobby windows. Then he got in the car and peeled away into the night.

The restaurant let out a collective sigh. Music started playing again in the background, servers returned to their tables, and the sounds of dinner resumed. It was like surfacing for air after being submerged in cold water.

Carter sat down on his stool and turned back toward the bar. The ice in his drink rattled against the sides of the glass as he swirled it around before downing it. "Tim, another one, please," he called out.

Tim mixed another drink for Carter and poured me another whiskey. He was wise enough not to mention anything about the exchange with Dustin.

I took a few minutes to look around the bar and pool deck. A man and woman sitting by the pool were leaning over their table and whispering to each other. The woman kept looking in our direction. I waved at her when we made eye contact. Her head jerked forward, and she tried to busy herself with the dinner plate in front of her.

Carter said something to me, but I didn't hear him. "Tell me about yourself, Billy," he repeated. His voice was surprisingly calm considering the events of the past few minutes.

"What do you want to know?" I asked.

"You tell me. I think most men would have high-tailed it home by now."

I took a sip of whiskey, unsure of what to say. I hated talking about myself. "I like to drink, and I like the open road." It sounded childish, even to me.

Carter snorted. "Sounds like the qualifications of a writer."

I looked at the whiskey in front of me. "It can be a curse."

"How does a man become a writer, or a journalist, or whatever it is you do?" Carter asked.

It was a simple question without a simple answer. I suppose I became a journalist the same way most people settle into a career, with blind ambition at first and then a growing lack of time and motivation to change. Carter chuckled knowingly when I said this.

"How long ago did the blind ambition disappear?" he asked.

"I don't know. Sometime after I realized everyone is the same, and sometime before I couldn't just sleep off a hangover."

"That must have been a long time ago."

"It feels like a long time ago."

I glanced past Carter at Jaselle. She had fallen silent again after her brief display of strength. I hoped she would find the courage to fight back again in her captive life.

"Have you found anything in your investigation of my son's death?" Carter asked.

"Possibly," I answered. "It sounds like Jordan was working with some shady individuals, including Dustin."

Carter didn't flinch at the accusation. "And you think those shady individuals murdered my son?"

"Possibly." I pointed to my temple to show my battle wound. "One of them gave me this cut. But as of now, there's no evidence they were here on the night of the party, which probably means the killer was someone closer to home."

Carter looked at my forehead longer than he needed to. "I'm sorry that happened to you, Billy," he said in almost a whisper.

"Hey, just part of the job," I said, trying to sound casual about getting my head caved in. "Like Dustin said, someone was bound to get me, eventually."

"What's your next move?" Carter asked.

"I need to go back to your office."

"What do you think you'll find there?"

"I need to ask the agents a few questions regarding Jordan's personal life."

Carter stared at me, trying to read my thoughts. Jaselle also looked up, but she dropped her gaze again when we made eye contact.

"My office is open to you anytime," Carter said with a tone of finality.

He gave me his phone number and told me to call him if I had any new information. I thanked him, and we drank whiskey until I was seeing double and Tim closed down the bar.

25

I woke up the next morning in a foul mood. My head was pounding on the inside and throbbing on the outside. The cut above my eye was a collage of dark colors. I tried to take a shower but felt like I was going to throw up in the confined space. Either my head injuries were worse than I thought, or Carter and I had drunk the entire stock of whiskey at the Blue Swan. I swallowed a handful of meds and left the motel without eating breakfast.

I knew something was wrong with my jeep the moment I saw it. Both tires on the driver's side were flat. I walked around to the other side, already knowing what I'd find, and of course, all four tires had been slashed. I went back into the Swan and asked the desk clerk to call a tow truck. After a few minutes, the dispatcher said a truck would arrive in an hour. I slumped down onto the lobby cushions and tried my best not to look like I'd spent the night sleeping in a ditch.

An hour and a half later, the tow truck pulled into the parking lot. The driver whistled when he saw my jeep. "Jeez, man. What'd you do to piss someone off?"

"You should see the other car," was all I could say.

I climbed into the tow truck and hid behind a pair of sunglasses. The driver introduced himself as "Dan the Truck Driver" and whistled all the way to the tire shop. The rocking and rolling of the truck reminded me of being on a boat again, and I had to focus on the car ahead of us to keep my stomach intact.

Two hours later, I paid the tire mechanic a thousand dollars I couldn't afford to lose. He handed me my keys, said the car was like new, and told me to have a great day. I wanted to curse him for taking my money so jovially, but I didn't. Instead, I drove to the Carter Real Estate Company like a madman, cursing every hippie on the sidewalk and every person smiling in their car. I cursed the sunshine, the wind, and the cloudless blue sky.

When I arrived at the office, I stomped up the stairs and pounded on the glass door. Jackie was standing in the office area behind her desk. I kept knocking on the glass until she walked to her desk and remotely unlocked the front door.

"Billy! Hi!" Jackie half shouted as I threw open the door. She looked behind her to see who else was watching. "I didn't know you were coming in today. Is everything OK?"

"Good morning, Jackie," I replied gruffly. "To be honest, I'm not OK. Over the past week, I've pulled a dead man out of a pool, barely avoided a pair of rattlesnake fangs, been assaulted and almost kidnapped, and had my tires slashed. So, no, everything is not OK."

"Oh my God, Billy. That's horrible." Her voice sounded concerned, but I couldn't tell anymore if it was genuine concern for me or concern about what my investigation was uncovering. "You said kidnapped?"

"Yes. Kidnapped. I don't recommend it; it was not a fun experience."

Jackie didn't respond.

"So now I need you to come clean," I continued. "And I need everyone else in this office to stop lying as well."

"What do you mean?" Her tone shifted from concerned to cautious.

"Someone in this office knows what happened to Jordan. In fact, someone here is probably the murderer, and everyone else is covering for them."

I glanced past Jackie toward the office where the agents were. Charlie's head shot up behind his desk like he was watching a predator at the watering hole. Matt was standing next to Charlie's desk; his usual smug grin was nowhere to be seen.

Jackie didn't turn to follow my gaze. Her eyes remained fixed on me, the fury I had witnessed on Catalina Island flickering again across her face. "Billy, this is not the way to handle any suspicions you may have," she said.

"So how should I handle it then, Jackie? Should I accept that Jordan got what he deserved and just let it go? Because that's what everyone keeps telling me." I felt my own anger rising again. I don't know why, but seeing Jackie and hearing her tell me how to handle my suspicions made my blood pump even faster.

"Billy, everyone obviously wants to know who killed Jordan," Jackie said. "But you can't blame them if they're not crying themselves to sleep over it."

"So let me get this straight. Someone murdered a man you spoke to every day, a man you built a career with and partied with, and you don't feel any sort of way about it?"

"That's not what I said, Billy. Please, be professional," she scolded.

"I am nothing but professional," I growled back.

Her voice dropped to a harsh whisper. "Listen, Billy, you have no right talking to me like this. I have tried to help you as much as I can."

"Do you know who Jordan was seeing besides Kylie?" I asked quickly, hoping to catch her off guard.

Jackie twitched, then narrowed her eyes. "I didn't know he was seeing anyone else."

"Kylie seems pretty certain that Jordan was meeting up with someone else and using the other agents as his alibi."

"This is news to me," Jackie said. "I never heard Jordan say anything about another girl."

"Did he ever ask you to go out on a Friday night?" Part of me felt guilty for implying such an accusation to Jackie, but I was tired of playing games and wasn't sure if I had been playing hers this entire time.

"Are you asking me if I was the girl on the side?"

"Well, someone has to know where Jordan was going and who he was seeing. And you seem to know everything that goes on around here."

"Damn you, Billy," she spat in a whisper. "I am not someone's side piece, and I am not a killer." A wildfire blazed behind her eyes. Still, she didn't order me to leave the office or cause a scene in front of watchful eyes.

"Fine," I said. "Then who knows?" It was the only thing left to say. I wanted to believe her, and I wanted to apologize, but a voice in my head wouldn't let me do either.

"Ask the boys," she said, then sat down in her chair and turned to her laptop, ending any further conversation between us.

I walked past the desk and headed to the back of the office. Outside the windows, the beaches were full of life and happiness. It felt like a different world from the one inside the office, with its artificially cold air and dream home advertisements.

"Alright, gentlemen," I said, stopping a few feet in front of Charlie's desk. "It's time to start telling me what you know. It's only a matter of time before the shit hits the fan around here, and everyone gets covered in it."

The men looked at each other, maybe questioning what the other knew or confirming that their alibis were straight. They had formed a partnership against me, either in crime or for moral support. Neither responded to my comment about getting covered in shit.

"I only have one question for you guys, and then I'll be on my way," I said. "Did Jordan tell either of you who he was seeing besides Kylie?"

Matt was the first to speak. "Billy, we have no legal obligation to answer your questions. You are not the police." His facial muscles curled into the smug grin they had grown used to wearing.

"That's true," I said. "But if I report what I know to the police, I'm pretty sure they'd take you down to the station for more serious questioning."

Charlie's eyes widened as he looked at Matt. The grin faded from Matt's face. I felt a flicker of triumph as I watched the corners of his lips turn down.

"Charlie, do you know what's happening in the empty houses your company is listing?" I asked.

Charlie flinched when he heard his name. He looked up at Matt for reassurance, who looked down at Charlie and shook his head like a father standing over his son. "Don't answer that, Charlie," he said, then turned his yellow-tinted gaze back to me. "I think you've mistaken yourself for what you really are. You write words on a page, and you think that makes you immune to interfering in other people's lives. But in reality, you're nobody. You know nothing. And you have no right or assurance coming in here with false accusations."

"You're right, I am nobody, and no one really cares what I write. But the moment I go to the police, this place will be crawling with reporters and podcasters who have a million followers, and there will be nowhere to hide anymore."

My words hovered between us like toxic gas. We remained silent for a minute, each considering the legal and safety ramifications of exposure.

"Why are you here then, and not at the police station?" Matt asked. "What do you want from us?"

"I want to know who else Jordan was seeing."

"He wasn't seeing anyone else."

"Then why does Kylie think so?"

"I don't know. That's a question for her."

I looked back at Charlie. His face had lost all trace of color. "*You* seem pretty close to Kylie," I said, letting the hint of accusation creep into my tone. "She must have come to you with her suspicions."

Charlie shook his head feverishly. "No. No, she never said anything like that to me." He looked up at Matt again, but Matt didn't silence him this time.

"Did it make you jealous that Kylie chose Jordan?" I asked. "You treated her so well. You picked her up when she needed a ride. You photographed her career. You'd probably drop everything you were doing and be at her door in a minute if she called. But, still, you were nothing more than a friend to her. Maybe even less than that—"

"Stop, please," Charlie tried to interrupt meekly. I knew my words were crushing his soul. Part of me felt sorry.

"Maybe I've been looking at Jordan's death the wrong way this entire time," I continued. "Maybe you couldn't handle seeing Kylie with Jordan anymore, so you decided to get rid of Jordan."

"No, it wasn't like that," Charlie muttered.

"What was it like then, Charlie? Because right now, you've got a pretty strong motive for wanting Jordan out of the picture."

Charlie suddenly slapped the desk and stood up. His cheeks flushed red. "No! I didn't kill Jordan." For a brief moment, his anger overtook his anxiety. It didn't last long, though. He looked around like he was surprised to find himself standing, then sat back down and put his head in his hands.

I let his self-pity wash over him for a few seconds before continuing. "I'm sorry, Charlie, but you still haven't told me anything to discredit the theory."

Charlie took a deep breath and lifted his head from his hands. "I... care for Kylie. I wouldn't do anything to hurt her, but Jordan didn't deserve her."

"Why not?"

"He didn't care about her. He only wanted to brag about having a model girlfriend."

"Was he cheating on her?"

"I think so. But I'm not positive."

"Why do you think so?"

"I overheard Jordan talking on the phone a couple of weeks ago. He didn't know I was in the room. He asked if they could meet at a bar called Eastbound again."

"Maybe he was talking to Kylie."

Charlie shook his head. "He wasn't. Kylie and I went to a movie that night."

"Maybe he was talking to a friend."

Charlie shook his head again. "Jordan said he was excited to see them. I don't think he would have said that to another guy."

"You have no idea who he was talking to?"

"No."

The front door swung open, and we all turned to look as two massive security guards entered the office. One of them pointed at me, then both men charged toward me. I thought I felt the floor shake beneath their boots. I raised my hands to show I was harmless, but they grabbed me under my arms and dragged me toward the door.

"It's alright. I'm leaving. I'm leaving," I said as my heels scraped across the floor.

"Shut the fuck up," one of them commanded. I listened.

I glanced at Jackie when we reached the front door, but she didn't even look up from her computer. The men carried me down the stairs and threw me on the sidewalk like a bag of trash.

"Next time will be a taser," one said. They crossed their arms and waited.

I stood up with as much dignity as I could and brushed off my clothes. I thought about blowing the men a kiss, but decided my face had already taken enough abuse in the past few days. By the time I reached my jeep, a new wave of excitement had replaced my morning hangover. I thought that in another life, I might have been a good Philip Marlowe. I also thought a drink sounded good right about now.

26

I stopped by the police station before heading to Eastwood. Detective Pratt met me in the lobby. I told her I needed information, and her eyes narrowed as she silently debated our journalist-detective relationship. I must have passed the test, though, because she told me to follow her to her office.

"What can I do for you, Mr. Burnes?" she asked, as she pointed to a chair at her desk.

I sat down, and she leaned against the desk next to me, forcing me to look up to make eye contact. "Have you pulled Jordan's phone records?" I asked.

Pratt snorted. "What makes you think I'd give you that information?"

"I thought we were a team?" I said, flashing my best smile.

Pratt did not look amused. "This is a real-life criminal investigation, not one of those murder mystery games. As I mentioned earlier, this is a one-way street when it comes to information. You tell us what you know, not the other way around."

"All I'm asking is if you pulled Jordan's phone records. I think he was meeting up with someone other than his girlfriend. If we can verify that, it might give us a lead." I was doing my best to sound diplomatic. Too much forcefulness would likely get me thrown out of the station and kicked out of Pratt's good graces.

Pratt considered my words for a moment before replying. "You're saying that Jordan was cheating on Kylie, and Kylie knew about it?"

"Yes. And I'm hoping his phone records will confirm that."

Pratt looked at me like I was an imbecile. "Wouldn't that give Kylie a motive?"

Her logic made sense, but in my experience, murder was typically driven by intense emotions like passion or anger. Kylie wasn't capable of feeling enough emotion to wish harm on others.

"I don't think she did it," I said. "Their relationship was all but over, and she was OK with it."

Pratt walked around her desk and sat down in her chair. She shuffled around some papers and then tapped her fingers on the desk. It was a bit annoying how often she paused to think before speaking. "And why would she tell this to you instead of the police?" she asked. "We interviewed her yesterday, and she didn't say anything about Jordan allegedly cheating on her."

"Maybe it's my charm," I tried to joke, but Detective Pratt didn't laugh. She just stared at me until I spoke again. "Or maybe she's had unpleasant experiences with the cops."

Pratt's face broke into a lopsided smile. "Everyone's had unpleasant experiences with the cops. But Kylie didn't seem fazed by us at all. She was calm and composed, maybe even a bit calculating."

"But do you think she is capable of stabbing a man in the back with a samurai sword?" I asked.

"I can't say for sure," Pratt replied. "I've seen a lot of things on this job that I never thought were possible." She paused for dramatic effect. "And there are some things I still need to believe in, but rarely see, if I'm going to survive." She crossed her arms and leaned back in her chair.

During my time as a journalist, I met quite a few detectives who had lost their faith in humanity. They were mean, callous, and didn't have the time to care about the people affected by crime. Detective Pratt was not one of those detectives.

"So, can you at least tell me if there was anything odd on Jordan's phone?" I asked. "Something that would support Kylie's hunch?"

Pratt didn't respond right away, of course. Her gaze once again seemed to weigh my character. If she had known my past, it probably would have tipped the scales in the wrong direction. Finally, she spoke. "You know, even though you're in the media, you have a friendly face, Mr. Burnes. I have half a mind to believe you actually care about finding Jordan's killer."

"Believe it or not, I actually feel sorry for Jordan," I replied. "No one cared about him when he was alive, and no one cares now that he's gone. That's a sad way to live and rest in peace."

Pratt nodded in agreement. "We didn't find anything unusual on Jordan's phone. But he could have had another one we haven't found yet."

"You searched his condo?"

"Yes, but aside from discovering he was a slob, we didn't find anything noteworthy."

"What about his desk at the office?"

"We searched that as well. Again, nothing noteworthy."

I was disappointed to hear that the police hadn't found another phone. If Kylie was right about Jordan seeing someone else, then he had done a good job of hiding it.

Pratt must have recognized my disappointment. "Perhaps Jordan didn't need a phone to communicate with another girlfriend," she said.

"That could be true," I said. Then a thought made my stomach tighten. "Especially if it was someone else in the office."

"Which would be Jackie Alcantar or Leah Donatelli, correct?"

My mouth suddenly felt very dry. All I could do was nod in response. Had Jackie really been playing me this whole time? Had she led me on a wild chase to uncover the agents' smuggling scheme and hide her involvement in Jordan's murder? If that were true, I'd lose my story and my job.

Pratt must have noticed something on my face. "You look like you have some thoughts about the women in the office, Mr. Burnes."

I took a breath to center my anxiety. "Both women claim there was never anything between them and Jordan. But I don't know whether that's true or not. I thought I had a good read on Jackie, but now I'm not sure about her or her motives. Leah admitted that Jordan made a pass at her, but she denied it went any further than that, and I'm pretty sure she's involved with Matt."

I told Pratt about seeing Matt touch Leah's leg during the poker game on Catalina. Pratt absorbed the information with raised eyebrows. "You are a treasure trove today, aren't you?" she said. "That sounds like another possible motive."

"Maybe. But why would Matt be jealous if he already had the girl?"

"Maybe Leah wasn't as saintly as she claims."

Pratt was right again, of course. Leah didn't seem to mind using all of her resources to get what she wanted. Maybe she had played the two men against each other, or used them both, and one of them got jealous.

"Since you're still talking to me, does that mean I have permission to continue investigating?" I asked.

"I wouldn't say it like that, Mr. Burnes. It means we aren't arresting you for interfering." I hoped she was joking, but she didn't crack a smile. "I need you to agree that you won't release any information you find to the public, and you need to report to me before you do any more gallivanting around."

"Deal," I said out loud. "No way, lady. I'm way past asking permission to gallivant," I thought to myself.

"And don't go around claiming you work for the police department."

I laughed at her joke, but stopped when I realized she wasn't kidding. "I don't think it would help if I did."

"Good. Then we have a deal." She reached across the desk and shook my hand like we had just completed a high-stakes negotiation.

San Diego loses its postcard appeal the farther you venture from the beaches. A couple of miles inland, it looks like any other city in America, except for a few scattered palm trees. An hour's drive east, and you don't even know the Pacific Ocean exists.

I took an exit off Highway 8 and stopped for gas. A Mexican kid, who couldn't have been more than sixteen, was pumping gas into an old diesel pickup truck. He wore a cowboy hat and stood with a confidence that comes from years of hard work. An old man sat in the shadow of the station with a sign asking for beer money. His skin was gnarled, and his clothes were ragged. He didn't look up as I walked past him into the store. I bought a tall can of beer and some gas from the woman behind the counter. She had deep crevices in her face that looked like the patched clay of a dried-up lakebed. On my way out of the store, I dropped a dollar in the bum's cup. He didn't raise his head or make a sound.

I drove with the windows down through the residential neighborhoods on my way to Eastwood. The houses here were small and flat, their front yards cluttered with everything that couldn't fit inside. Groups of children patrolled the streets like hyenas in the bush. The sun beat down hot and heavy. There were no ocean waves or cool breezes to escape the heat this far inland. This was the edge of the desert and the last stop before humanity succumbed to the sun.

Eastwood sat on a dusty patch of dirt on the outskirts of town. You could sit on the hood of your car in the parking lot and gaze across the desert at the mountains beyond. From the outside, the bar looked like a simple black box with Christmas lights wrapped around the corners. The name "Eastwood" was painted in plain white letters on the front. But the people standing in front of the door looked young and hip. Their cowboy boots were new, their plaid shirts were clean, and their faces were bright and fresh. Their trendiness seemed to be a deliberate mockery of the surrounding desert and local community.

I parked and waited for the dust cloud to settle before walking to the bar. One of the young guys standing outside the entrance had a cigarette in his hand, but he held it awkwardly, as if it were his first time smoking. One of the girls said, "Welcome, friend," as I walked past. I instantly hated them even more.

The inside of the bar looked like a country bar that had been taken over by the hipsters. Keg handles, beer bottles, and string lights hung from the ceiling. An oval-shaped bar with shelves of fancy liquor was positioned in the center of the room. A raised dance floor took up almost half of the remaining space. The whole thing felt like a weird concoction of microbrews, handlebar mustaches, and line dancing.

I grabbed a stool and waited for the bartender to come over. He was a cheerful-looking guy around my age with a loose afro and gray streaks in his beard. "Hey. How's it going?" he asked with a friendly smile. "Can I get you something to drink?"

"Whiskey, please. No ice."

He set a glass in front of me and poured just enough liquor to cover the bottom of the glass. "My name's Buddy," he said with another smile. "Let me know if I can get you anything else."

I wondered if Buddy was always this happy. Had he discovered some secret the rest of us hadn't? Had he found perfect contentment serving drinks on the edge of the desert? I hated to admit it, but overly happy people always made me cautious. "Thanks, Buddy," was all I replied.

I sat there for another half hour, trying not to let my bias against bad mustaches and weak drinks influence my judgment of the bar. I understood why Jordan would pick a place like this. It was far enough from his usual hangouts that he wouldn't run into anyone he knew, but still trendy enough to meet his bloated standards. Still, there must have been some risk if he was really trying to hide. The patrons here were socially conscious people who enjoyed talking and meddling in others' affairs.

A group of guys standing around one of the tables was slapping the table and singing along to some pop song. They seemed to be in the full throes of a good drunk, even though it was early afternoon. A group of women was a few tables away, drinking almost as heavily. They looked older than the guys, but they sang and laughed with drunken youthfulness. I figured it was just a matter of time before the groups merged and sparks flew. Their afternoon promised delight and drama, infatuation and regret.

After my third drink, I decided it was time to start asking questions. Buddy finished helping a couple at the bar and then walked over, still smiling wide enough to show the world that his life mission had been accomplished.

I tried to return his smile, but it felt awkward. "Hey Buddy, does it get crowded here on weekends?" I asked.

Buddy draped his towel over his shoulder and looked around like he was imagining the weekend crowd. "Oh, yeah," he said, pleased with what he was envisioning. "We have a DJ, and the dance floor gets busy."

"Do you work weekends?"

"Every weekend for five years."

"I think my friend was in here recently, but I haven't been able to get in touch with him," I said, trying to sound casual despite the seriousness of my words. "Could I show you a picture of him and see if you recognize him?"

Buddy's cheerful mood turned cautious. I could see his mind jumping from the deeply ingrained habit of customer satisfaction to the natural instinct of wariness. "Maybe," he answered. "Is your friend in some sort of trouble?" The smile had disappeared from his face.

"He might be," I lied. As of three days ago, Jordan was free of all his troubles.

"OK, sure," Buddy said, regaining some of his spunk when he believed he was helping a legit cause. "Show me a picture."

I showed him a profile picture of Jordan from the real estate website. Jordan was turned in a three-quarter pose, wearing a dark suit and a confident smile. His blue eyes sparkled like he had just committed highway robbery and gotten away with it.

Buddy leaned over the bar to look at my phone. "Yep. I recognize him. He has been coming here for a while now. Isn't he the guy who's been on the news? He got stabbed, right?"

"Yes, he did."

"Then why'd you say he went missing?"

I scolded myself for the stupid move. Of course Buddy had heard about Jordan's murder; the whole city had. "I'm sorry," I said. "I guess I figured you'd be more willing to talk if you thought you could help the situation."

Buddy frowned. "If I can't help the situation, then why are you asking me about him?"

I glanced down at my empty glass. I wanted to ask for another round and a chance to restart the conversation. But by this point, Buddy was spooked. Leave it to me to make the happiest guy in the world frown. "OK. I'll shoot it straight," I said. "I came to see if this guy had been meeting anyone here recently."

Buddy looked at my white T-shirt. "Are you a cop?"

"No. I'm an investigative journalist."

My title did not impress Buddy. "I don't think I should talk to you, man."

"Listen, I'm trying to help figure out who killed this guy. His name was Jordan. His girlfriend thinks he was seeing someone else on the side, and I think he was meeting that person here. If that's true, and we can identify her, it might help solve Jordan's murder."

Buddy didn't respond right away. He looked around the bar again, this time searching for backup or moral support. "OK," he said finally. "It's not like I'm doing anything criminal, right? I'm just checking to see if I recognize this girl?"

"Exactly. Nothing criminal at all. All I need is a yes or no."

Buddy nodded. "OK, I can do that."

"Awesome. Thank you. But first, can you just tell me how often Jordan came in? Was he a regular?"

"I wouldn't consider him a regular. He only showed up on Friday nights, but not every Friday—maybe every other one."

"Have you seen him lately?"

Buddy's face scrunched up in thought. "Yes, I think he was here last week or the week before, if I'm not mistaken."

"Was he with anyone?"

"He always met the same girl," Buddy answered. "They never showed up together, but they always left together. I assumed they were dating."

"What made you think that?"

"They were always on top of each other at the bar, always touching each other. And they liked to dance. The girl probably would have danced all night if your friend, Jordan, hadn't pulled her back to the bar every few songs."

I pulled up a picture of Kylie from her social media account. "Is this the girl he was with?" I asked, showing him Kylie's picture.

Buddy shook his head. "No, I don't think so."

The hairs on the back of my neck stood up. Kylie was right. Jordan had been driving to the edge of the desert to keep a romance secret.

"I'm going to scroll through some more pictures," I said. "Stop me if you recognize anyone who looks like the girl Jordan was meeting." I started scrolling through pictures from the real estate company and Jordan's social media accounts, hesitating over each one as Buddy leaned in to examine it. Finally, he stopped me.

"I think I recognize her," he said, pointing at the phone. He squinted for a closer look. "Yep, that's the girl who met him here."

I felt a rock sink into the depths of my stomach. I couldn't believe I had been so blind and easily manipulated. After days of wading through jealousy and lies, the truth was finally emerging as a picture blurred with deception and torn by rage.

27

I drove west, back toward the beaches and the American Dream. A radio weatherman said the wind and swell would continue for another day and praised our fortitude for surviving this long. I turned off the radio. I was really getting tired of weathermen complaining about beautiful weather.

Traffic was light on the weekend, and I arrived back at the Swan an hour after leaving Eastwood. I parked in front of the motel and started toward the lobby entrance, but stopped short of going inside. The security camera above the entrance had recorded Jordan leaving the motel on the night of his murder, but never reentering. The only assumption was that he had accessed the building another way. I walked around the side of the motel, searching for any other doors or windows that Jordan could have opened and slipped through. There was an employee door on the back side of the building, presumably a trash and delivery entrance, but it was locked. There were no windows on the first floor, and all the windows on the second floor appeared to be guest rooms. The bottoms of the windows were at least twelve feet above the ground, and Jordan would have caused a racket if he had climbed through a window and crawled over a sleeping guest. I figured someone could have pushed out a window screen from inside and let him in, but it still would have been a long way off the ground.

After completing a circuit around the exterior and finding nothing significant, I looked up and down the street for anything that might have beckoned Jordan's attention. It was early morning when Jordan left the Swan. The streets would have been empty of people and cars. He could have met someone, but Detective Pratt said they found nothing suspicious on his phone. Calling or texting someone to arrange an early morning rendezvous would probably count as suspicious.

I started walking south on Rosecrans Street out of impulse. A few blocks down, two bars faced each other from opposite sides of the street. Their signs indicated they both closed at midnight. Even the bartenders working late would have been gone by the time Jordan passed by.

The bars and shops along Rosecrans ended abruptly, and the street continued into an upscale neighborhood. Multi-story homes with big windows and panoramic views of the bay crawled on top of each other up the side of the peninsula. I turned right to avoid walking through the neighborhood and trudged up the hill along the edge of wealthy homes. After a few blocks, I turned right again, heading north from a higher point on the slope. The houses here were smaller than those behind me and appeared to have left their prime in the fifties.

I turned right once more and walked down the hill toward the Blue Swan. The entire building was shaped like a horseshoe, with the open end facing away from me. The left side and back wall were flat from the ground to the roof, but the right side of the horseshoe featured an exposed hallway that extended from inside the horseshoe to the doors of a few outer-facing rooms. Cars filled the parking lot below the exposed hallway. It occurred to me that Jordan could have climbed onto the roof of a car and then pulled himself over the railing to the second floor, thus bypassing the security camera at the entrance.

I hurried back to my jeep and pulled it around to the side of the motel, parking as close as possible so that the hood was directly beneath the outdoor hallway. I got out and looked around for anyone walking by or smoking a cigarette. The coast was clear, so I climbed onto the hood of the jeep and then onto the roof. The top of my head was now level with the hallway, and my outstretched arms reached halfway up the railing. If Jordan had indeed gone this way, he would have had to climb onto someone's car and then pull himself over the railing. I wondered why he would do such a thing, but then pushed those thoughts aside because trying to understand the motives of someone jacked up on synthetic energy was pointless.

After another quick glance around, I grabbed the railing with both hands and tried to pull myself up. I cleared a few inches and then dropped back down, praying the roof of the jeep wouldn't cave under my weight. On my second attempt, I tried bringing my right knee to my chest so that my toe would fit under the bottom of the railing, but I couldn't get my foot high enough and dropped down again.

I shook out my arm muscles, which had grown weak from years of sitting behind a computer, and took three quick breaths. Then I grabbed the railing and pulled myself up again. This time, my right foot tucked under the railing. I used it to push myself high enough to slide my left toe under as well. Then I stood upright, took another breath, and climbed over the railing, landing in the hallway as gracefully as Simone Biles at the Olympics. If anyone had been in the hallway to watch my performance, I would have bowed.

Jordan very well could have entered the motel the same way. With a mix of alcohol and stimulants coursing through his veins, it might not have even been difficult. I was about to head down to the lobby when I spotted a fire escape ladder at the end of the hallway. I walked over to see if it was operational. Its bottom rung was roughly level with the top of the railing, and its top rung reached up to the roof. If Jordan had been determined enough to get this far, then a quick hop and climb up to the roof wasn't inconceivable.

I looked over the edge of the railing before attempting the climb myself. The twelve-foot fall to the hard pavement below would probably break an ankle, at least. To hell with it, I thought—what's a little more peril to an investigative journalist with his career on the line? I put my right foot on top of the railing, kicked myself up, and reached out to grab the ladder. Luckily, my hand wrapped around the cold metal of the rail. Unluckily, my center of gravity now hung in the space between the railing and the ladder. I slowly extended my foot out, got it balanced on one of the rungs, and pulled the rest of my body over to the ladder. After that, I scurried up as fast as I could.

Only when my feet were firmly planted on the roof did I look down again. The ground was at least twenty feet below. I panted until my heart rate slowed and silently cursed Steve and Corbin for forcing me to cover this story. When all of this was over, and Corbin had paid me for saving the magazine, I was going to buy a handle of whiskey, order every kind of takeout imaginable, and not leave my apartment until my bruises from this week had healed. It was a great thought, and it made me feel a little less tired.

The roof was flat with a two-foot parapet wall around the perimeter. Several AC units and pipes were scattered across the rooftop, and an access door was at the far end. I headed toward the door, hoping to get down without risking any more broken bones, but I stopped halfway. A piece of an apple was sitting at the base of the parapet. It was wilted and covered in gray fuzz, but appeared to have been neatly sliced in half. A rush of excitement shot through my nerves. Jordan had been on the roof, and he'd brought his sword with him.

Thankfully, the rooftop door was unlocked and led to a short flight of stairs. I left the door open to let in the sunlight and followed the stairs down to a storage room, where another door led to the hallway. I was about to step out when a door in the hallway opened. I quickly ducked back into the storage room as the sounds of a family passed by. When it was quiet again, I peeked into an empty hallway and then stepped out, closing the door behind me.

I went down to the lobby to talk to the desk clerk. He was a young guy with a pimply face and nervous twitches, and even though he had been working the past two days, I still had to glance at his name tag every time we spoke.

"Hey, Glen," I said. "I need to ask you for a big favor."

Glen's back stiffened. "Hi, Mr. Burnes," he said in a boy's voice. "What can I do for you?"

"Would it be possible to pull the guest log from the night of the murder?"

Glen instantly broke out in a sweat. His eyes darted around for help, but there was no one in the lobby to hide behind. "I'm sorry, Mr. Burnes," he wheezed. "I'm not supposed to give out information like that."

I nodded and gave him my best smile. "I understand. But this information could really help solve the murder. I suspect that the man was on the roof when he was stabbed, but to get up there, he would have had to climb over the railing on the outer hallway. It's possible that someone staying in one of those rooms saw something."

Glen still looked nervous, but he seemed a bit more intrigued. Maybe he was the kind of person who looked for gossip to impress his friends. Maybe the idea of solving a murder added excitement to an already dull life.

"Glen, this could really help the investigation," I said again. "Hell, when it's all over, I may even write about your help solving the murder."

Glen took a few deep breaths. "OK. I can pull up the records for each room, but I can't print anything. I'll just read their names to see if you recognize them."

I pointed a finger gun at him. "That's a great idea, Glen."

The kid smiled and punched a few keys on the laptop in front of him. "We are looking for the night of the 26th, right?"

"That's the one."

He clicked some more buttons and was about to say something when the lobby door swung open. Glen looked up with wide eyes, and I slowly turned to see who had entered. It was an elderly couple wearing big straw hats and T-shirts that read "I love San Diego." I waved awkwardly at them. They waved back and smiled like they had rediscovered a fresh spark of life on the sunny beaches of Southern California. Then they walked through the lobby and out the door to the stairs leading to the guest rooms.

I looked back at Glen. "You were about to say something, Glen."

"Yes. OK," he stammered, bouncing his head to motivate himself. "There are three rooms on the outer side. I'll pull up each one and read the name of the registered guest staying there that night."

The kid read off three names, but I didn't recognize anyone from the party. "OK, here's another question. I'm assuming you need a key card to access the roof, correct?"

Glen nodded. "That's correct."

"But if Jordan was already on the roof, he could have gotten down without a key," I said, mostly to myself because I had just proven it could be done. "But he would've had to recruit someone to hold the door while he ran to get his sword."

Glen looked at me as if he was waiting for me to give him the answer. "Glen, can we look up one more room, please?" I asked. "Who was staying in the guest room closest to the storage room on the second floor?"

"Let's see. That would be room 204," Glen muttered as he typed on the computer. "Here it is," he said after a moment. "According to our records, the room was checked out to someone named Ross Carter."

28

I drove to the beach to gather my thoughts and calm my nerves. I parked at the back of a crowded parking lot and walked past tailgate smokers and tourists packing up for the day. A group of surfers was unloading their boards from the top of an old-school Volkswagen bus and rushing toward the beach. I followed them to the sand and found a vantage point on a dune that divided the beach in half.

The beach to my left was filled with families and lovers. Kids splashed around in the late afternoon waves, laughing when they belly-flopped into the water. Romantics huddled together on beach towels, waiting for the sun to set. Artists sat with sketchbooks in their laps, trying to capture a feeling that couldn't be expressed on paper. A father held his young daughter's hand as she tiptoed toward the water. A wave came in, and the water swirled around the girl's ankles. She splashed from one foot to the other and smiled up at her father. I wondered if Jordan had ever looked at Carter like that. Then I wondered if someone would ever look up at me like that.

The beach to my right was filled with dogs and their human companions. Some dogs leaped through the surf, others chased each other through the sand, and one spun in circles chasing its tail. All but a few, who cowered behind their owners' legs, were smiling only as dogs and children can, running at full speed just to feel life's breeze.

A pod of pelicans floated overhead, observing life below from the safety above. They moved slowly, seemingly content to let the ocean breeze carry them home. I wondered whether they could recognize the differences between people from that high up, or if we all looked like ants scurrying through the sand, hunting for a morsel of happiness in this great big world.

A surfer rode a wave to shore until he stalled in the whitewash, then dropped to his belly and paddled the rest of the way in. He carried his surfboard through the sand and up the path to the showers. His day was complete, but he would be in the ocean again tomorrow, and the day after that, and the day after that.

The ocean breeze filled my lungs and flowed through every part of my body. I wiggled my toes in the sand to feel its coolness. I think I could have stayed there forever, with the kids splashing in the surf and the dogs running on the beach, letting the spirit of the place warm my soul. But the sun crept relentlessly closer to the horizon, and I understood that the greatest happiness in life is being with the people you love.

29

I called Carter, expecting him not to answer. To my surprise, he did. I asked if we could meet somewhere to talk. He said to meet him at his house, gave me the address, and hung up.

I stopped at Jerry's on my way. There was no cover charge today, and the bar was filled with grunge-looking guys dressed all in black. The tattooed bartender who called me "Hun" set my whiskey down in front of me and asked about my plans for the evening.

"Getting ready to go home," I said.

She smiled knowingly. "It's always nice to go home after a long one."

I ordered another whiskey and gulped it down. As I walked back to my jeep, I tried to convince myself that I was a good journalist and a confident person. I had endured a hellish week of violence and poor choices to reach this point. Backing down now would nullify it all.

Carter's house was just a few miles down the beach, but the line of cars on Sunset Cliffs Blvd. moved at a snail's pace. By the time I pulled into his driveway, I was feeling anxious and claustrophobic. Carter was sitting on the second-story patio like a king overlooking his domain. Only the two-lane road and cliffs separated his front door from the expanse of the Pacific Ocean.

"Good evening, Carter," I said as I stepped out of my jeep and peered up at him.

"Hello, Billy. I thought I might see you again soon," he said without getting up from his chair.

"This is quite the place. How's the view from up there?"

"Like a dream. Come on up, the front door is unlocked."

I let myself in and paused in the entryway. The inside of the house looked like the final product of a home renovation show. Everything was new and immaculate. Looking out the living room windows, I could see the sun sinking toward the ocean.

I found the stairs and went up to the second story, where the patio door had been left open to let the ocean breeze cascade through the home. I coughed to announce my presence on the patio. Carter looked over and smiled with a lifetime of knowledge and exhaustion. He held a cigar in one hand and a drink in the other. A half-empty crystal decanter sat on the table beside him.

"I'm happy to see you, Billy, believe it or not," he said, pointing to a seat at the table.

"Why is that?"

"Because the world is full of idiots and thieves, but I don't think you're either one."

"I guess I'll take that as a compliment," I said, sitting down in the cushioned chair Carter had pointed to.

Carter smiled. "You should. I don't give compliments lightly."

I looked out over the vastness of the ocean and sky. The sun was swelling in size and intensity as it inched closer to the horizon. It was one of those sunsets that made you feel small, human, and powerful all at once. It was one of those sunsets you could see a thousand times and still not be able to look away.

"Want a drink?" Carter asked, offering me his glass. "Finish it, and I'll refill it."

I looked at the half-full glass of alcohol and questioned accepting it. But what's a man worth if he doesn't live by a code, even if that code is never turning down a free drink? I took the glass from his hand. "What is it?" I asked.

"Twenty-five-year-old single malt scotch."

I downed the drink in a single gulp, my face twisting at the taste.

Carter laughed. "Taken like a true drinker," he said, taking the glass from me.

We sat in silence for a minute, both lost in our own thoughts and sense of demise. Carter smoked his cigar and watched the sunset, while I leaned back and let the scotch flow through my veins. For a fleeting moment, we were bound by the mutual solace that we had finally reached the end of the ride.

Carter was the first to speak. "The sun has to set on all of us, doesn't it?"

"Yes, it does," I replied.

"We just hope it's as beautiful as the one we see now." He raised his glass in salute to the setting sun.

"Yes, we do," I said. "Is yours going to be this beautiful?"

Carter lowered his glass and looked at me before turning back to the view. "This might be my final one."

"What made you do it, Carter?" I wanted to add "to your own son," but didn't.

Carter didn't respond for a long time. I let him stew in his emotions and waited for him to reply. "Anger. Jealousy. Arrogance. A mix of all three," he finally said.

"Did you know about Jordan and Jaselle?"

"Yes."

"How long had it been going on?"

"For a couple of months. Jaselle tried to deny it at first, but they couldn't hide it from me. They were sloppy."

"Where is Jaselle now?" I asked, glancing around for any signs she was home.

"I don't know, and I really don't care," Carter answered.

"Does she know what happened at Jordan's party?"

"Yes. But she won't talk. She would lose all of this." He waved his hand over the patio and the view of the ocean. "She likes shiny things, and I give her shiny things."

"But why stay with her? I'm sure there are plenty of other beautiful women who would do anything for this life."

Carter snorted. "I have to, now. Like I said, she likes shiny things, and now I buy her shiny things to keep her quiet. It's the best relationship I've ever had."

It was a sad thing to say, and I wondered if the young man from Texas who had dropped everything to move out here with his wife would have agreed. "Last night, when I had drinks with you two, did Jaselle already know what'd happened?" I asked.

"She did."

"And you still made her come?"

"Yes."

"Why?"

"Because I can." His words were sharp and arrogant. He was the puppet master, and he wasn't ashamed. He was a man who had accepted his faults long ago and maybe even found pride in them now.

I couldn't help but feel sorry for Jaselle. I remembered the look on her face as she stirred her drink in a whirlpool at the bar. It was the look of a trapped animal that had already given up fighting against her captor.

"It was you who put the snake in your bed on Catalina, wasn't it?" I asked.

"I admit, not my best idea," Carter said, a hint of a smile crossing his face.

"What was the idea?" The image of the snake's fangs inches from my hand made the hair on my arms stand up.

"I didn't have much of a plan. Events just sort of forced my hand," he said as if fate had taken away his freedom. "I was walking on the trails above the camp and found the snake curled under a bush. I've been handling snakes since I was a kid, so I hurried back to the cabin, grabbed a pillowcase, and went back up the trail. The snake was still there. I knew that rattlesnakes on the island were more defensive than those on the mainland, and man, was it a bitch to get in the pillowcase." He paused to smile at the memory. "I left the pillowcase in the bathtub while I made a little concoction of booze and Dramamine for Jaselle. Then I dropped her off with Leah, put the snake in the bed, and waited."

I had to admit, wrestling a rattlesnake into a pillowcase was impressive, even if it demonstrated an unhinged level of crazy. "Why?" was all I could ask.

Carter smiled again, proud of his failed attempt. "If Jaselle was bitten, then she got what she deserved. If Leah pawned Jaselle off, then it would make Leah look suspicious, and eyes would turn away from me."

I nodded in agreement, then scolded myself for doing so. "I have to say, it had me fooled. I thought the snake was meant for you."

"I'm good at what I do, Mr. Burnes," Carter said. He paused a moment to let the depravity of his statement sink in. "Now, let me ask you a question. If you assumed I had killed my son before you came over here tonight, why did you come alone? What made you think I wouldn't do the same to you?"

"Do you have another samurai sword or a snake hidden under my chair?" I asked because I didn't have a better answer.

Carter leaned forward in his chair. "No, but I have other tools."

I held his gaze while I thought about the foolishness of coming here alone. "I guess I'm just tired," I said after a moment. "I'm tired of watching my back. I'm tired of chasing you down. I'm tired of getting my ass handed to me. I came here tonight so we can end this and I can go home."

"What if I had to keep you quiet, though?" Carter's eyes flashed again; his mouth twitched at the corners.

"Then we would have made a final scene worthy of the movies: two men, locked in combat, on a patio overlooking their final sunset."

Carter laughed and relaxed back in his chair. "I like you, Billy. It's unfortunate we met at this junction in our lives."

I realized I had been squeezing the armrests of the chair and relaxed. "So, what made you do it?" I asked again. "Why that night? Why in public?"

Carter took a slow sip from his scotch and thought about the questions. "I didn't plan it out, if that's what you're asking. The opportunity presented itself, and I let my emotions get the best of me."

It was another bullshit answer. His lack of moral responsibility showed how far he had fallen as a man.

"I figured out how to get onto the roof at the Swan. Is that where it happened?" I asked.

Carter nodded once. "It is."

"So, Jordan climbed onto the roof, got back down through the employee door, and then what?"

Carter took a drag from his cigar and exhaled before answering. "I was smoking a cigar outside my room when he came through the employee door. I could tell right away he was on something. He was twitchy and bug-eyed, and a wave of disgust washed over me the moment I saw him. And you know what, that's the last image I have of my son; not of him on the pool deck, not of watching the sword go through his back, but that one—the image of a bug-eyed junkie." He paused to catch his breath and take another drag of the cigar. "I gave him everything he ever wanted. I gave him fortune and identity. And he repaid me by becoming a junkie and sleeping with my wife."

I didn't know how to respond to a man who had passed his worst traits to his son and then murdered him because of who he had become. So I asked if he'd share another sip of scotch. He handed me his glass, and I gulped down the contents once again.

"Why give him the promotion?" I asked after the harshness of the scotch had dissipated.

"I wanted him to know that I could give him everything and then take it all away."

"You were going to fire him?"

"I was going to go to the police with whatever scheme he had with Dustin."

"You didn't know about the drugs?"

"Not entirely. But I had my suspicions. And I wasn't going to let the company I built from the ground up be mutilated and torn down by someone else."

"Wouldn't the police shut down the company?"

"That was the plan."

I nodded as I finally understood. "Burn it all down yourself and then sail away, huh?"

"Sounds pretty nice, doesn't it?"

I couldn't fault him for his sentiment. Hell, I had thought about disappearing hundreds of times in my life. Chasing the horizon on a beautiful yacht would be a good way to go, but the trail of murder rarely leads to happy endings.

"So after Jordan came through the employee door, what happened next?"

"He told me to hold the door while he went to grab something," Carter continued. "So I held the door for him; I don't know why. And he came back with that goddamn sword and a handful of fruit and said he wanted to go up to the roof. I asked him why, but he just pushed past me to the stairs. I followed him, and by the time I got up there, he was already swinging the sword around like a maniac. As a father, it was embarrassing to see my son cranked out and hopping around. But I tossed him a couple of pieces of fruit and then asked to give it a shot. He handed me the sword, and when he turned around, I stabbed him in the back and shoved him off the roof."

A normal person might have shed a tear talking about the death of their son at their own hands, but Carter spoke matter-of-factly, his actions justified by the image he held of his son. "So you followed him up to the roof," I said, "but you didn't plan to kill him?"

Carter took another long drag on the cigar. He lifted his head, blew the smoke into the air, and watched the wind carry it away. "No. But I'd been so mad at him for so long that I couldn't stop myself. His mother and I grew up in the country. We worked hard and left behind everyone we knew to move here. And once we got here, I worked my ass off to build the company. Jordan thought that because he was my son, he was entitled to take the reins, but he didn't have what it takes. He was smug and cocky and wanted everything in an instant. The only reason he had a job was because he was my son. And then he thought he could replace me."

Carter worked up his emotions as he rambled on. Maybe he was still mad at Jordan, or maybe he was angry at everyone else for not understanding the plight of the rich and powerful. I pulled out my phone and sent a quick text to Detective Pratt while he spoke. He didn't notice.

"OK, so how did you get down from the roof without us noticing?" I asked. "The desk clerk saw Jordan land in the pool and went out to check on him. I was out there pretty quickly after that."

"I was stunned after Jordan went over the edge. I heard the splash when he landed in the pool, but I couldn't move. Then someone called down to the clerk. It was you, but I didn't know it at the time. After a second, my body loosened up, and I went down the stairs and waited behind the storage door until the hallway was quiet. Then I just opened the door and slipped into my room. Jaselle was asleep in the bed. I changed my clothes and sat at the desk until Jackie knocked on the door to inform me about my son."

Carter watched the families gathering on the cliffs as he spoke. I wondered if he looked at the fathers carrying their sons on their shoulders and felt anything. I wondered if there was any inner longing for the family he lost or the family he never had.

"Do you regret doing it?" I asked.

Carter looked at me and took a deep breath. "I feel like I should be sorry. What kind of monster kills his own son? But honestly, even when I was standing over Jordan's body, I felt nothing. And I haven't missed him since."

"Why tell me all of this? The police haven't figured it out, and as far as I know, there's no solid evidence against you. Why confess?"

"I guess I'm tired too," Carter said. He was calm again, as if he were at peace with his decisions, however horrible they may have been. "What more does a man have to live for when his son is dead and his life's accomplishments are being desecrated by the people he tried to uplift? I have fought for too long. And now I'm tired."

It seemed to me that Carter had justified his actions and accepted his fate. Whether he deserved a special place in purgatory for killing his own blood was no longer our decision, but a jury of his peers would decide the future of his natural life. Lawyers would paint a picture of a maniacal old man who had broken up his first marriage at the first taste of wealth and then murdered his son when his son slept with his second wife. The story would dominate the tabloids for days. Carter would forever be remembered as the man who devoured his son.

I left Carter sitting on the patio while he watched the sun set on his world. I could hear police sirens approaching as I got into my jeep and pulled out of the driveway.

30

In the end, I told Detective Pratt about my experience at the stash house. She said her team would bring in Dustin and Matt, although she wasn't sure what the police could prove against them. She was upset that I hadn't told her about it earlier, but relented when I reminded her of my help in closing a murder case.

I stayed up until the early hours of the morning writing the story. It had all the elements readers would love: drugs, violence, wealth, and deception. But what intrigued me most were the raw human emotions—those that weren't premeditated or orchestrated. I was interested in why we each have a savage instinct to climb over our fellow man, even when that fellow man is family. It was the same instinct that had corrupted the border, and it culminated in the destruction of a family that owned and sold the American Dream.

I checked out of the Blue Swan the next morning. A new guy working the front desk jumped to attention and asked me how my stay was. I told him I would never forget it. He looked confused but smiled and thanked me for choosing the Blue Swan.

The storm that had been gathering offshore for days was finally making landfall. The weather forecasters would be pulling their hair out, and the tourists would be cursing their luck. It was going to be a gloomy, miserable day, and everything I could wish for. Before getting into my jeep, I took one last look at the Swan. Its neon blue sign stood out against the gray clouds like a beacon calling home weary travelers. I thought of Jordan's blank stare as he looked up at me from the pool deck and everything that had been exposed by a few seconds of violence. Then I pulled out of the parking lot and didn't look back.

I drove slowly down Rosecrans Street in the opposite direction I'd come a week ago. The street was mostly empty of life. The hippies had gone back to their hideouts for the day, and the families were tucked away in their hotel rooms. The only people outside were the bums, who squinted at the sky in confusion—it wasn't supposed to rain in the land of eternal sunshine.

I stopped at the diner where the old man read his books alone. He wasn't there, but the same waitress was. She welcomed me back and laughed when she said they still didn't have any beer. While she took my order, Carter's face flashed across the TV screen above the breakfast bar. The news anchor said authorities had arrested Ross Carter for the murder of his son and that more details would emerge in the coming days.

The waitress shook her head and sighed. "These rich people always think it's their money that's going to watch their back. But look at them now. One is dead, and one is in jail. And they're family!" She shook her head again and grabbed the menu off the table. "Look at me, talking about other people's lives again," she said and laughed at herself. "I'll bring your coffee right over."

Half an hour later, I was on the freeway heading north. I called Jewels to tell her I loved her and that I was coming home. The sign by the side of the road read five hundred miles to Sacramento. Jewels told me she loved me and to get home safely.

website: **billyburnes.com**

contact: **billyburnes916@gmail.com**